The Talented Ms. Rosemary Evening
Book #1 of the Snow Globing Series

Paranormal Romance
By
Cindy Night
(Cynthia Night)

Published by Clocktower Books
San Diego, California

Contents

Publisher's Preface 2017 Venti Edition

What is the Clocktower Books Venti line? And what is the Venti Blush subset of our Venti line? These are shorter print books, usually accompanying e-book editions from Clocktower Books.

Into the late Twentieth Century, driven by factors dependent on technology, publishers generally published fiction in one of two printed modes: short stories (magazine format) or novel format (book format).

Unfolding digital technologies are creating a wealth of new opportunities for readers and writers, often side-stepping backward corporations in New York who continue to cling to outdated print paradigms and heavy-handed methods. Readers will be eager to discover new reading pleasures, while writers are happy to sidestep the tyranny of five giant, lumbering, foreign-owned trade conglomerates, and offer exciting new literary and fun works.

Part of the new paradigm, since paper magazine and print are no longer the only game in town, is that old lengths no longer matter. A digital (e-) book can be any length, as long as it meets the highest standards of writing and editing. Many of us involved in Internet publishing have advanced degrees in English and Business Administration, among other disciplines, and are often better suited to bring exciting new creative writing to readers who are tired of spending money and being disappointed.

In that vein, we launched the Read-a-Latte concept years ago, which is a concept suggesting that you don't need to pay outrageous, artificially pumped up prices for same-old product—especially when it comes to the exciting and fresh new world of e-books. Yes, there's a lot of new material out there, and anyone can publish a 'book,' but we're not just anyone and these aren't your average books. Trust us or try them (trust but verify).

John T. Cullen, publisher of Clocktower Books, has come up with a new name for a line of shorter books. At one time, these were considered an unwelcome oddity in publishing, referred to (while making a face) as chapbooks.

We're done making faces here, except smiley faces.

Ventis are the new concept in books. Ventis will be the new, flexible length type of fiction—for the price of a latte—with pricing to match that of a cup of coffee rather than paying for an overpriced and often underwhelming brick from New York.

The print edition of The Talented Ms. Rosemary Evening, launching the Snow Globing Series of literary erotica, is our first offering in the Venti Blush erotica line.

The word 'venti' is Italian for 'twenty' or 'winds.' We idea is that a Venti should be longer than a short story, so we draw a line in the sand at 20,000 words, but Ventis can go anywhere in length, as can their twin e-book. Think of the Venti as somewhere between a short story and a novel, to use outdated print terminology driven by Gutenberg technology from the 1400s.

By a totally outside coincidence, you may travel to the lovely city of Ventimiglia in Italy (Mild Winds) or you may sip a venti coffee in your favorite bookstore. Whatever you do, we're with you.

Do check out our coming line of shorter Clocktower Venti Novels, including Venti Blush subset. Thank you for joining us at John T. Cullen's Café Okay, the coffee-themed bookstore of Clocktower Books, and enjoy.

Prego! Thanks.

Publisher's Preface 2015 E-Book Edition

Welcome to the fascinating and imaginative worlds created by San Diego author Cindy Night (Cynthia Night), the latest addition to the small and select stable of Clocktower Books talent.

Cindy has promised us a series, and she's hard at work on the next sexy paranormal romp in the dream world. As she explains it, we sleep one third of our lives. Those eight hours a day are filled with adventures in a dream world we never remember with any clarity when we return to the wakeful world.

Future titles will include *Night City Blues*, *She's Not Easy*, and other great concepts in this same cosmos. Only *espish* (ESP-like) Talents like Rosemary Evening, Janna, and the irresistible Joe Street can operate at will in the dream world, the way the rest of us function in our daily lives. I take that back. More correctly, let's say that the Talents are superheroes in that world.

Nothing from their wakeful world leaks into the dream world, so they know nothing about their wakeful selves. Conversely, as you already know, *what happens in your dreams stays in your dreams.*

Some Talents are broken people whom life has treated cruelly (divorce, a lost child, cancer, horrible car crash, you name it). Other Talents are happy go lucky, sexy, beautiful men and women in dreams as well as daily life. Both types find healing and betterment in the dream world. As they prosper in the dark city of dreams, their wakeful selves heal as well. They leave behind fear, guilt, inhibition, poor self-image, and all the other demons that plague us wakeful types. While they save the world night after night, their wakeful selves grow stronger and more self-assured.

In the shadow of Clocktower Books (online since 1996, providing exciting books for avid readers since the dawn of the World Wide Web), we have created the fictitious Clocktower Institute (CTI), whose director is the charming Dr. Joe Street whose life becomes entwined with Rosemary's in the city of dreams. There is some soap opera here, since Rosemary suspects that Fanna, her beautiful guide, has already been intimate with handsome, vulnerable, bad boy boss Joe Street. As with Torchwood or Continuum, to name just two great TV series, the Snow Globing series will bring many other exciting titles.

What is Snow Globing? Forget anything you ever heard. Picture one of those beautiful glass globes with a tiny city in it, glowing in a bluish light under a silver dollar moon. Shake it, and pale flakes slowly drift like snow among thousands of tiny windows. Imagine all the dream world soap opera going on in those buildings. Now picture CTI (and the U.S. Government) inserting secret agents (our Talent, starting with Rosemary, Fanna, and Joe, plus other great characters yet to come) into those drizzly streets, foggy corners, with flashing limos and honking taxis and music drifting out of bars. Each Snow Globing mission will be a great story we can savor in our wakeful world--and perhaps catch a glimpse as we drift off to our dark slumber in the Sexual Healing Garden of dreams. Let the adventures and healing begin. Above all, let's have fun with this wonderful imagination and Cindy Night's amazing creations. Nothing quite like this has ever been done before.

--JTC 31 Aug 2015.

Chapter 1. Doorway to Healing Dreams

Your doorway," said the shimmering figure as she led me from pain to glory. "Welcome home to your dream life, Rosemary."

When you cross through the portal of dreams, you become free for the first time--from hurt, from guilt, from fear, from grief, from terror, or worse. Here is where you begin your new life as a free human being. Here, in your dreams, you can finally be really you as you were meant to be.

We spend a third of our life sleeping, and much of that dreaming. We don't remember the dream world, except as a vague memory of good or scary dreams. Don't call waking the real world--the dream world is just as real on its own terms.

Dr. Joe Street and the Clocktower Institute (CTI) of San Diego rescued me from the horrors of what my waking life had become--I know nothing of it here in the dream world, except I do know that in dreams we heal. In dreams we fix the waking--not the world, but ourselves, and that changes everything.

When I crossed the bridge into the dream world as a Talent, I became Rosemary Evening. I don't even know my real name in the waking world, but I know everything I do here--every action I take--makes life better for me on the other side.

In dreams, you meet new people. You make friends, you fall in love, you have hot steamy passionate sex, you lose all the inhibitions and other obstacles you create in your waking life, and you heal. That's why CTI calls their campus in Banker's Hill, near Balboa Park, 'your sexual garden' or 'your healing garden'--right out of the late Marvin Gaye's sweet songs.

It was to be all of that, and more. It is wonderful. You would hardly know from this inauspicious entry that I would become (as my admiring and delectable boss, Dr. Joe Street, brilliant bad boy of dream street, would soon call me; lots more about that, and him, later) the Talented Miss Rosemary Evening--agent extraordinaire of the dream world, a talented paranormal who would change the furniture around in the universe.

Think of it this way. We sleep one third of our lives. We probably daydream and idle another third of our lives. The remaining third we deal with survival--work, spouse, children, traffic, drive by shootings and other random, insane violence that terrifies us. We deal with death--our own, and of our loved ones--the unbearable. We deal with back stabbers, thieves, bosses from hell, spouses from purgatory (sometimes, the unlucky among us), and need I go on? When I learned of my espish talent, and how I could explore the dream world that is so vast in our lives, I was ready. My life was not a happy one--I'll leave it at that. I'm not even sure why. You're not supposed to know, over here in this dream world that you occupy eight hours a day.

I remember just about nothing of the waking world,

and very little of my transition, except that I was trembling for unknown reasons. I can't what dark emotions might have followed me up to that gateway. I'm sure they included anger to the point of rage; pain to the point of agony; fear to the point of terror; guilt to the point of self-loathing; and all the usual things that broken people bring with them to the garden of healing. Honestly, I think it was all of the above.

The shadowy staff of the Clocktower Institute (CTI) determined I have a major talent--I am very espish. That refers to extra-sensory perception (ESP) except this has nothing to do with telepathy, levitation, or other unproven paranormal arts. This has to do with dreams. The espish, like myself, have the power to move about in the dream world. We have the power to change lives--our own and the lives of others we meet in that alternate reality. We spend a third of our lives in that world. There is much more in there than some vague memories over morning coffee and daylight. Some say that life itself is but a dream. I won't argue that point either way. I only know that I have the gift of a wonderful power--which works only on the other side. This is how my story began, what became of me, and how I helped others to find the same peace. Much of it is through sexual healing.

Your dream world is your personal sexual garden. Most of us wander through there in darkness, afraid and confused of our own passions and desires. We walk through gloom, though we smell roses. We wish we could stop and see, but most of us don't have the espish ability to anchor ourselves and be an active player in that shimmering, floating world. I'm lucky that way (surprise, after nearly thirty years of undistinguished, average life). Oh yeah, we do have daylight in here. It's one surprise after another. You'll be amazed. Stick with me and learn all that I can tell you--I am still learning, also. There is so much to tell.

The good doctors and guides at CTI first tested me because I had a hard time in my daily life. Someone--a guide, an espish, a cognoscenta--figured I might be good dream material. Maybe it was my friend Fanna or someone like her. I would think she encountered me in her dreams and spotted my talent that I knew nothing about. In some dream, I probably floated through a darkish tavern in some city, surrounded by wolfish and threatening men and coyote-like women who scared the hell out of me with their grinning teeth and knifish eyes. Picture foxes and wolverines in business suits, holding happy hour drinks, and figuring ways to cut and rip each other psychologically for narcissistic self-gain. Argh--but somehow, Fanna or someone spotted me and knew. There goes another espish type. Let's recruit her before she slips down the rat hole of unknowing daily existence. Maybe I also drank too many glasses of Chablis to numb the pain. Maybe I smoked cigarettes or jee or who knows what. I have no idea. I just know I felt like I was living with a thousand pound concrete mill wheel on my back--all that unhappiness. I really don't even want to know what oppressed me so much.

I don't know what--a messy marriage, a tragedy, just bad luck--all I know is that once I crossed into the dream world under their coaching and guidance, I became a free person. The transition is not a permeable membrane. It is like a solid wall you pass through. What happens on one side stays on that side. What happens on the other side stays on that side. Never the twain shall meet. Which is fine. And the healing you do in the dream world will change your waking life for the better. See, once you experience freedom and joy, you will never settle for anything less. Once you become a whole person, with self-worth, you can meet members of the opposite sex who are also healthy and complete. You can experience fulfilling, balanced love (and sex, yeah, lots of it, fueled by joy and passion). Inwardly, though you remember nothing of your dreams when you are awake, you will never allow yourself to fall back in a ditch. Your inner joy and satisfaction become a balance wheel that keeps you on track.

This story is not about my waking life. In my dreams, like now, I know nothing of my waking life except that I am an adult woman about 29 years old with a lively, active brain and a good education. I have a revving sexual appetite that evidently has been frustrated to no end in my waking life--probably due to inhibitions, fears, guilt, timidity, and anything else I could name here as I sit here entering this journal into my virtual memory base.

Yes, I am writing this from the dream side of my life. I am sitting in a corner in a little apartment--all very cozy and kind of quietly dark--with a window open and a curtain blowing gently. It's a dream efficiency--I have a kitchenette corner, a dining corner, and a small Pullman-style bed nook in the main room; and a full bath adjacent. A balmy evening breeze wafts in from the Pacific Ocean, here in the city of San Diego. I am on the twenty-somethingth story of a high rise, where I have a small apartment (just for my sleeping and dreaming hours). I think I probably have a house in the suburbs with a lawn and a picket fence and a yellowish coach lantern over the driveway. I think I probably have it all, except that I have been miserably unhappy. Even in your dreams, you carry a vague awareness of your waking life. For me, it is a dull awareness of yelling and conflict, of being yelled at by a handsome but angry and rather mean-spirited man whose name might as well be Mud for all I know here. I prefer it on this side. My healing is ongoing. I have a guide--Fanna, an elegant and intelligent woman just a few years older than myself, who cares about me and always knows the right thing to say. It's still a struggle over here, but I am making progress. It's often a lot of fun, and actually hilarious (I should have mentioned up front) so it's a million laughs, like my first move when I became free. I saw a line of men in gym shorts, bending over a barbecue picnic table with their plates, and I ran down the line grabbing each by the ass. You know how we used to take a clothes pin and fasten a matchbook to our bicycle wheel when we were kids, and it made this RRRR sound like a motor. That's what I felt like--you'll see in a moment. Freedom is crazy and exhilarating.

What was I running from? Nothing happy or good, I would imagine. I was in such psychic pain that I was trembling and sobbing when Fanna led me across into the dream world to begin my healing. I imagine I was on a couch at CTI in their staidly ritzy, Victorian-era Bankers' Hill offices near Balboa Park. I have no idea. I don't know, and I really don't want to know, what misery I was freeing myself of. I simply didn't know then, and I still don't really know now. But it doesn't matter. What is important is what happens on the dream side, which changes your life on the other side. You never go back to victimhood, to oppression, to fear, to inhibition, to guilt (over nothing, really). You become a female gorilla let out of her cage. ROAR! See? I am woman and I can ROAR all I want, dammit. I will roar, and I do roar all I want. Actually, I got over the roaring part pretty quickly and started to ask Fanna and the other people in my dreams: What now? How can I help others? There is so much to do. There are so many poor souls to help--men and women alike, who need this espish therapy. I am an adept, come to find out. Maybe my story will help you feel better.

Once you cross through that portal from waking to dreaming, you remember nothing of the other side. When you are dreaming, you have little to no idea about your real life, except that it is probably not as happy and empowered as the dream world. When you are awake, at the same time, you remember nothing of your healing dreams. The motto is: What happens in your dreams stays in your dreams. That's how this works.

I was shaking like a lost puppy. My face felt as if it were streaked with tears, and my eyes ached from being washed in hot salty tears. I had no idea what my deep grief was all about, and that ripped sense of loss, but I still felt the pain. I felt like the dry heat after a house fire has been put out.

"The past is behind you now," she said comfortingly. We were two females, standing in a confined space with a high ceiling that seemed to taper off into dreams--maybe even into dark space sprinkled with stars.

My only answer was a dry, racking sob. I had run out of tears.

"What are you feeling?" she said. Her name was Fanna, an otherworldly handle on a tall, wraithy female with long ice-blonde hair, a pale lovely face of indeterminate race, but human species, and gentle--that was all I cared about.

She was a few inches taller than me. I am average everything--looks, height, cleverness, you name it. As I have come to accept myself, I lost weight just be feeling good about myself. I have a nice body with good curves in all the right places. I am that woman men only notice when the beautiful, shouty blondes leave the room. My hair (which I could turn to gold or white in my dreams, if I wished, but I choose to be me) is a rich, dark forest brown with hints of amber and glints of sunlight. My face is pretty in an understated way, with clean lines and large, happy dark eyes. My mouth is full and laughy (pardon how I make up words; I really don't give a fuck, okay, and here you don't need to). I have a good tongue, and kiss well and long. The men I have kissed always want to come back for more. They want to feel me, running their palms over my thighs, their fingers over my cheeks and forehead as they gaze into my eyes. I also know what dresses I look best in. I prefer to wear loose fitting, dark, richly tailored dresses in cottons or silks, colored anywhere from plum to merlot. It makes me look more alluring and mysterious. I have power in the dream world, even though I am so very average. It's all about attitude.

So there we were, during my transition. I was a shivering, sniveling wreck with swollen eyes and runny mascara. My lips quivered endlessly as I blubbered in misery. I forget if I kept my arms folded around me for dear life, or if I kept reaching out to steady myself on Fanna's elbow (something to cling to in my desperation).

Fanna's large eyes sparkled with golden slivers, while the irises seemed to change shades of color in a range from light greens to light blues and a lot of rainy gray in-between. She wore a long, straight gown that fit her slender form, showing only white slippers wrapped in gilded ribbons on the concrete floor. Were we in a parking garage? Was I dreaming? Of course I was dreaming.

"I feel--" I started to say as we just began to entered. That's when I really started crying. See, that's the first part of release--the waterfall of tears and grief, letting go. It's the moment when you cannot go on. It's the moment when you want to throw yourself on the ground and die. Only I wanted to live, and Fanna would not let me down. My eyes ached, so I must have been crying a lot. They burned, but I could not remember. I was all in. I started to sag to my knees, feeling woozy, but Fanna caught me in a surprisingly strong grip on a steely arm, slender as it might be, and almost transparent like pure ice. No, there was warmth under that hard skin. She was an ancient spirit, but young as the day was new. I collapsed against her tender form, into her healing embrace.

I don't know how long I sobbed blindly before the tears ran out, maybe dried by a baking heat in my cheek bones. My eyes burned from the grief I felt. My soul felt torn into rags with loss.

When I grew still, she gently released me so I stood on my own two feet. I felt strong now. The air was fresh and sweet, as if we were on a mountain top overlooking pine forests on a spring day.

"You are ready to move on," Fanna said. She pointed behind me, and I turned to look. Behind us was a tall, narrow closed doorway, two wings, made of something like dull clean copper. It was engraved with all sorts of enigmatic designs that looked like an otherworldly alphabet. High up on the door frame was a sign in my own language, which read: "Awaken."

"What does it mean?" I asked, feeling embarrassed at my newborn emptiness, a void of knowledge.

"It means there is a new life out there when you wake up."

"So where are we?" As I asked, the space around us became more clear. We were in a concrete looking shaft, almost a well, or an elevator. Ahead of me was a door like the other, only it said: "Dream."

"You will never be the same," Fanna said, raising her hands. Slowly, the Dream portal swung open. At first, it revealed only roiling white vapor.

"Am I dead? Is this heaven?"

Fanna laughed. "You are asleep, Rosemary. This is your very own special dream world. This is where your healing is going to begin, right now."

"What happened to me?" I asked, inwardly grabbing at shreds and snatches of a vanishing memory of terrible dark things. The awful things I had been through were evaporating, the way fresh wind blows in through a newly opened window and clears away fetid odors and smoke. Soon it is as nothing had been there, just this beautiful spring breeze scented with greens, with flower breath, with just a hint of warmth that penetrates aching bones and relaxes tight muscles.

"What happened to you back in your life is now a

stale, broken house of cards that has been knocked down and can never reassemble itself. You are free, Rosemary. You still have a long life ahead of you, and you can do anything you want. We are here to help you."

"We?" I asked, holding my hands awkwardly behind my back. I looked down. I am not so bad looking. I saw a reasonably nice, slender figure in a kind of almost velour, merlot skirt, a puffy white blouse with short, trimmed sleeves and tiny pastel flowers embroidered on the hems. Looking down, I saw strong, feminine legs with nice even feet trapped in soft black leatherish quarter heel shoes. Brushing my palms down over myself, I felt a soft but tight stomach (maybe a little puffier than I'd like) and behind me just a little more behind than would have been desirable, but firm and smooth. I was not wearing stockings or underwear. Reaching up, I felt my puffy, tear-swollen face. I used my fingertips to squeeze the burning hollows of my drenched-out eyes. Quickly, I ran my hands up over my head, feeling thick, straight hair captured in a cloth band. I felt a bit like Alice in Wonderland, in the old picture books, the way my hair fanned out and fell halfway down my back.

"We," she said. "We are your Helpers. Welcome to your Sexual Garden. This is your Sensual, Sexual Healing dream world. You need not worry about anything except being good to yourself and to others you meet here."

"There are others here?" I asked, suddenly self-conscious about my appearance and the lack of underwear. I could remember nothing about my life, so I had no idea if I'd been homely or overweight or dressed dowdy or who knows--a lot of frankly scared imagines flittered through my mind.

Fanna laughed. "Yes, there are others. Many of the souls you will meet here are Helpers. Others are Healing, like yourself. This is a hospital of dreams, we like to say."

"Do I get to go back?" I asked. "My life--"

"You will go back before you know it. Your life out there in the waking world is already better because the things that made it hurt are either gone or fading away. A lot of the things we worry about, including the pain in our past, is just weather."

"Weather?"

"Weather, Rosemary. Think of it as weather or not. We can choose to live under a cloud of bad memories, or we can choose not to. That's whether or not. Think of it this way. Memories are no different than dreams. They exist only in your head. So if you are asking--how can this be happening? Is this real? Think about it: your memories, including some very bad ones, are just like dreams in your head. Here in the dream hospital, we fix all that. When you grow into your new self, you will be able to control your feelings. You'll be able to blow your pain and sadness away, as the wind blows clouds away over the mountain tops, never to return. Did you know that clouds are mostly made of water, Rosemary?"

I had to smile. I'm not so dumb. "I know that." Why didn't I think of things like this to say?

"Clouds are made mostly of tears, Rosemary. You know what else is in clouds? Particles of dust and dirt. Think of shaking your pillow out, and all those icky mites fly away. When the sun comes out and shines her warm light into those gray old clouds, or even the big puffy white ones that are actually the most watery and tearful, filled with dust and must, that's when all the rain falls, that's when all the tears fall like they just did with you, and next thing you know, you are smiling with the sun herself."

"I thought the sun is a guy," I said.

"The sun is sometimes a guy and sometimes a woman," Fanna said. "It's all about mythology. These dreams are all about mythology. I can tell you this. In every culture there has ever been, the sun and the moon are opposite genders. For the Germans and the Japanese, for example, the sun is a woman and the moon is a guy. For most modern cultures, the sun is a guy and that lovely orb lighting the night sky is a mysterious beauty like the Mona Lisa in the painting."

Chapter 2. Into The Dream World

As Fanna spoke, the portal ahead of me (*Dreams*) swung wide open. I stepped out of the transition portal between waking and sleep, and stood in my own healing garden of dreams.

I felt like a girl, clapping my hands over my mouth and making wide, amazed eyes. They no longer burned. A couple of small birds like finches swooped down with fluttering, feathery wings, and sprayed something--eye drops, maybe?--into my eye sockets. For a few seconds, their little beaks looked like the muzzles of tiny water pistols in the toy store. I cried out with shock, then relief, and rubbed my eyes with my finger tips. The finches fluttered away into the blue sky, leaving a few fluttering downy feathers to prove they'd been there. My eyes felt wonderful now. I blinked, and looked out over green hills and valleys. I saw red clay-tiled roof tops on white houses in the distance, and a space that looked like a golf course sprawling in a flat land below me. A ribbony river glowed in distant sunlight.

"Is this for real?" I asked.

"Everything is for real," she said. "This is your dream, Rosemary."

"Is it safe to be here?" I felt disoriented and a little scared.

"The worst thing that can happen is you wake up."

"And the best thing?"

She nudged me with a girl-to-girl elbow and a wink, nodding her head a the golf course below, or football field, or whatever it was. A whole squad of the most gorgeous men in this dream or any other were running together around a jogging track. They wore only skimpy shirts and silky running shorts that showed off their glistening, sweaty muscles. A few had slight afternoon beard shadow. All were intent on their running, and did not notice me-- yet. They were very handsome. Feeling a rush of desire, I felt embarrassed and covered my face with my hands. But I peeked through my fingers.

"All of this is yours," Fanna said. "This is all in your dream."

I was still looking between my fingers at the leg muscles on those guys. Their shorts looked bulgy in front. Their arms were wiry as cables, sunburned, and slick with sweat in the mild sunshine.

For a crazy second, I wondered if I could turn up the heat. Like, make the sun warmer. Would their arms become even more slick? What else could I do here to make the time go by?

Fanna must have read my mind. "You're getting the right idea, Rosemary. Now comes the hard part. No pun intended. You have to learn to be gentle. These are real people, visiting you in their dreams. You have to be nice to them, as you would be in the waking world. Here, the difference is that everyone is in some stage of healing and discovery."

"What stage are you?" I asked.

"I'm healed," Fanna said. "I am a Guide, a Helper. I would hope that, when you are well again, you will come back to your dream world often and help the new ones who are still suffering from whatever bad things they went through in their waking life. We can't change our waking life while we sleep. But we can learn to master our minds and our emotions, and simply blow off bad people who are tormenting us in our waking state. That especially goes for all those useless memories of terrible men and terrible women who have hurt us in the past. You'll see how easy it is, once you get the hang of it. That's why we are all here together."

"It is making more sense," I said now. "I guess I had reached a point of no return."

"Your instinct is right. But we won't even go back there to find out. It doesn't matter if you were married to a man who was mean to you, or if we grabbed you off a tall bridge before you could jump, or if you were abused...Let's not even think about it."

"I don't want to," I said brightly, a grown woman, feeling about six years old at the moment. I felt the innocence of a child, and all that limitless potential ahead of me, before mean people and awful events could ruin everything.

"You will have many adventures here," Fanna said. "I know, because I am still having them, and I've been here longer than I can remember. When we wake, we remember who we are, and what our life is, but the pain grows ever more remote and dull, until we start forgetting it. We are reborn with these sensual and sexual dreams in the healing garden."

"Does everyone have the same dreams?" I asked.

As we spoke, the portal shimmered and evaporated behind us, revealing more of this dream world. Behind us sprawled a lovely, mysterious city with tall buildings, green parks, and drifting airplanes in a blue sky. To one side shimmered the rolling waves of a greenish-white bay fronting on the city's harbor.

"Everything is here," Fanna told me. "I will be your helping angel when you need me. You will dine with handsome men, dance the night away, and make love under the starlight."

"Oh.my.gawd."

"Yes. But you must never be embarrassed. You know how that airlock is tight as might. The one we just came through. Nothing penetrates in either direction. Your dream life is one hundred percent separate from your waking life. You remember nothing about this while you are awake, except a vague, warm new feeling of goodness that you have long not been used to. You will never feel bad about yourself again, Rosemary, and you never needed to."

I felt like starting to cry again, but nothing came out. My eyes were dry and bright. My body felt strong and firm, and I could not have trembled or shivered if I had tried to.

"Remember this," Fanna said. "This is the most important thing you must know."

"Yes?"

"What happens in your dreams, stays in your dreams."

"That.is.awesome." I could hardly speak.

Fanna nodded with wisdom and certainty. Suddenly I realized how full of her own secrets she was. She said to me: "Rosemary. You know that old saying about Las Vegas? Same thing applies here. What happens in your dreams, stays in your dreams."

With that, she took my hand, and guided me as we walked down a long, gently sloping grassy hill to the golf course or track meet and whatever else it was below. I heard a brass band somewhere, faintly, its pulsing music lilting on the wind whenever the breeze turned this way. I thought I smelled fresh beer and bratwurst, not to mention sharp mustard and maybe a fork full of sauerkraut over a sizzling barbecue grill. Or was that shrimp on the barbie? Or basted ribs? No matter. I had all the time in the world to explore this world and its many secrets--my dream world, my sexual garden, my sensual healing. This was a place where I could let it all hang out, never feel guilty, enjoy every pleasure as long as nobody hurt anybody. I almost felt a little frustrated. Why had nobody shown me this before? Why do we all live in so much guilt and fear and self-doubt? In the clarity of my healing dreams, it all seemed so obvious. How pointless spiritual pain is. How cruel is pointless guilt. I let out a wild laugh, made sail plane wings of my arms, and ran down the hill ahead of Fanna. I heard her laugh behind me--a languid, relaxed, been-there-done-that kind of happy exclamation. My new friend. But what about those guys at the track? Ah, they were all grilling now. I think one or two saw us coming, and nodded, with big manly innocent grinning mouths full of shiny teeth. Already, I was beginning to desire something more than a few hot shrimps; on my barbie, no less. Or in my barbie, not on it. Oh naughty me. I could feel so raunchy all of a sudden, so damp of thighs and sighs, and not have a shred of guilt.

Chapter 3. First Delicacies

As we drew near, the men were all huddled over the condiments table, holding paper plates brimming with tangy delicacies. Seeing a row of silk clad behinds, I looked at Fanna who kept pace beside me. I studied her flat, Nordic (I think) pale features, so pretty and exotic.

"Can I?" I asked. My voice was a whisper. That was the closest I'd come to shaking and trembling once again-- with desire, maybe even anguish, but not anything self-bad.

Her full mouth twisted into a knowing grin. "Not too hard. Don't hurt them."

So I walked along the row of men, grabbing their tight little buns with both of my eager, hungry hands. There is no describing it, since nobody has ever done such a thing (that I know of) in the waking world. The guys didn't even seem to notice. Their buns felt tight and muscular. Some were bigger than others. I liked the smaller, bunnier ones you could get into your palm and squeeze your fingers around. All those muscles, so compact and sweaty. Probably hairy under those jogging shorts, too. Some of them had these cute donut asses with a dimple on each side in the middle of the muscles--great to hold on to, but I was more into yelling WHEEEE and running down the line grabbing each bunny butt one by one.

"Easy on the balls," Fanna muttered through her teeth, into my ear as she swerved behind me. "Take your time. No rush. There are--what?--about twenty of them. That should last you a while. Their balls hurt if you accidently knock them. The buns are lovely, aren't they?"

"Oh I want them," I said in a hungry tone. After a lifetime of denial, I was like a starving animal.

"Remember the old saying," Fanna told me. "Don't spend all your buns in one store."

"Tell me again," I said. "I need to hear it just one more time to be sure."

"Don't eat all your buns in one score."

"Thank you." I hesitated, just a fleeting second. "Will I not be mortally embarrassed forever by what I get myself into here?"

Fanna shook her head slowly, and made a face as if I were a slow learner. "Rosemary dear, remember: what happens in you dreams stays in your dreams."

I stood holding a man's mountain oysters in my starving little paw, and looked at Fanna. The man was busy discussing baseball with another man, while they dipped into chicken bits and barbecue sauce, and he didn't seem to notice or care. I wanted to grab his shaft and make it hard, to see if I could arouse (no pun intended) his attention, but I wasn't that far along yet. My healing process would have a way to go. Also, that barbecue sauce smelled divine--just the right amounts of sweet (brown sugar), sour (vinegar), smoke (woodsy), and salty (sea salt). I was more hungry for men than for chicken tits.

Actually, I was more hungry for this new feeling of freedom. It was like being drunk on fresh mountain air. Talk about oxygen.

"Repeat after me."

"I am a kid in a candy store."

"No, Rosemary, that's not what I said." She was having trouble not bursting out laughing.

"I know," I said, punching her shoulder lightly with my free hand. "What happens in my dreams, stays in my dreams. I just want to keep telling myself over and over again, in case I lose my nerve."

"Or wake up suddenly," Fanna said. For a second, a dark cloud shaded her bright eyes.

I took warning from that, and let the poor man strut away holding a tasty, drippy chicken breast aromatic with tangy sauce.

Everything has its boundaries--even here. Of course, that makes it all the more spicy.

"You like it so far?" Fanna asked me. Somehow, a fizzy vanilla shake had appeared in her hand, with a squiggle of whipped cream on it, and a red cherry on top. You get used to this in the dream world. You can wish something, and it's the next thing that happens. Continuity isn't what you are used to in the waking world. One minute you're in the office, eyeballing Mr. Perfecto. The next minute you are in a hot tub at his mountain ranch, both of you stark naked and holding margaritas while curling your toes together. In the waking world (we don't say 'real world' to avoid confusing the issues) it would happen differently. There would be a lot of confusion, mixed signals, bated breath, hopeful sighs, will he or won't he. Then there would be an hour of traffic jams and who knows what else. Here in the dream world you simply float (not lurch) smoothly (usually) from wish to fulfillment, from desire to fire.

Fanna's ice cream was in a parfait glass, one of those

heavy old-fashioned ones. She sipped from a straw. Her lips had gone from snow-pale, almost bluish, to glossy red the color of that cherry (her cherry, I suppose, if everything in dreams has Freudian meaning). Anyway, about her lips--quick makeup job, huh? I wondered if I could get stuff like that; maybe a makeover, pampered by a sweet gay man who could not stop talking about his darling Roger or whatever. It is with gay men that straight women experience relief from men who prefer hen.

"Yeah," I said. "I am totally experiencing bliss. And anticipation."

"What are you anticipating?"

"Whatever happens next."

She blinked both eyes shut with contentment while holding her glass in both dreamy bluish hands and sipping. She was enjoying the hell out of that sweet drink.

"Something crazy," I said. "Show me the possibilities."

She blinked again, this time in acquiescence. "Okay, Rosemary. Something whacky. Here goes."

One instant I was standing there talking with her, and lusting after her milk shake.

Oh, I forgot to say that in dreams, you can eat or drink anything you want. You don't gain an ounce, and if you drink too many shlupps with your pupps there is no hangover.

The next minute, the whole scenery and everything had changed. Like wow, wowowowow.

That's how it goes in dreams. There are few transitions. Everything flows into the next.

Chapter 4. Got His Point

I was sitting at this outdoor bar in a park--in a dream, of course--sipping coconut milk through a straw from a porcelain shell. All I wore was a little paper napkin on my lap. Luckily I was a curvy, athletic, tight brunette in this dream, and my edges didn't hang over the leather-chrome dinette stool. The seat was one in a row of about twenty such stools bending around a boomerang-shaped surface covered with everything you'd expect to see on a bar, from nuts to cherries, a jar of pickled weeners, and a bowl of *sheeps* (those are chips imported from strange lands).

A chunky, pink man wearing nothing but a red bowtie sat on a suitcase, stroking his bass fiddle nearby, accompanied by a young blonde with thick eyeglass lenses on keyboards, while a crew-cut wrestler type gyrated over his drums, cymbals, and high hat with steel brushes making *chook-chook-chook* sounds, *ka-djing, ka-djong,* very jazz. Come to think of it, none of them wore anything but matching red bowties.

And, getting right to the point, neither I nor any other occasional indulger at the bar wore anything much as we sipped away and listened to music and enjoyed the sound of birds in nearby trees, a bubbling fountain, and a llama tied to a palm tree.

Speaking of palm trees, the waiter and the waitress, every time someone ordered another glass of coconut milk, would go with a pail and milk the nearest coconut palm tree. There was a whole herd of these palms over on a meadow under a Manhattan-like skyline. Some of them mooed as if we were in a dream. Which we were, of course.

Just then, a tall, knife-slender, gorgeous man in a tuxedo entered the park. He was achingly beautiful, with fine light-olive features atop a long neck, bony gleaming cheek bones, and large dark eyes like brandied coffee just wanting to be drunk out of. He had an expression of mystery, of night, of savage desire. I bet if I could lean over and run my nostrils lightly along the muscles under his shirt, he would smell of forest and wolf. He might even growl deeply at my attentions. When he smiled, as he undid his bow tie and threw it fluttering away over his shoulder, his teeth were like sugar and I wanted to slide my tongue in there to find his tongue. Our tongues would howl together in the moonlight. Somehow, I knew his name was Daniel. Guys like that are always named Daniel, which is a male name as smooth as a cream aperitif. Drink two or three of those and you could pass out backward on the lawn, losing your napkin for all to see your all and then some.

Daniel dropped his black tux jacket on the grass as he made straight for me. I gathered that, since it was my dream, I owned everything in it. At least, you'd hope so. I was to learn differently. You don't own it, you're just in it. It is a world all in itself, with its dangers and passions. It has its intriguing people and exhilarating events. You're just in it, which makes you a citizen of it, which means you own a piece of it and have a right to be there. You take what you can because you are meant to have it.

Daniel looked mysterious, haughty, almost heartless until I saw his crying need to be loved. He was a stallion (not a centaur, and not for real, just a manner of speech) fighting at the bit every inch of the way, but snorting and tossing its head and yearning to be tamed. And I was going to be the one with the lasso in that dream.

He tore his crisp white shirt off and dropped it behind him as he approached me with steely, wiry bare arms that rippled with muscles and sun-bronzed skin. Oh my was he bronzed. That boy must spend his week days surfing or lying on the sand. I couldn't wait to ask him as he came near. He unbuckled his belt, yanked it snake-like out of its loops, and tossed it over one shoulder as he strode toward me.

He mouthed my name, drinking the air around the syllables: "Carmella." My name always changes in dreams, but that is one of the more common ones. I am different in most of the dreams, which makes things more interesting. When I am Caramel or Carmella or Carmen, I am a caramel-colored Latin woman with dark glossy hair falling in rich waves over my shoulders. As I reached up with one hand to brush my hair from my eye on that side, which is a signal to a man that I am open to whatever, he raised a perfectly manicured beach boy hand palm up as if offering himself to me. As he stepped right up to the bar beside me, and signaled for a coconut milk to a young woman in a red bow tie who was just returning from the coconut herd with a full bucket, he slid his strong hand down my back and gave me shivers of delight and anticipation.

My worst nightmare just then was that I would wake up before his other hand could do whatever it planned with me. I was so ready. I was about to get his point.

I didn't wake up, but kept blissfully snoring away in the real world while having adventures in this lovely dream. We can only guess what happened next because the catch is, of course, you never remember what happens in your dream. Even if you think you do, you don't. Or you may bring back a false memory, just to keep you in the dark (so to speak). You get the point.

What happens in your dreams stays in your dreams.

I was to learn a great many things. We never stop learning, especially in the dream world.

The flip side is that you remember nothing about your waking life while dreaming, which is a total blessing about 99.99% of the time because nothing can be quite as intoxicating as a deep dream with a handsome surfer in a tuxedo. Or if you are that guy, your dream will have someone like me that you can chase after down a sandy beach under a strangely deep blue sky full of night stars and maybe a full moon. You get my drift.

I am telling you this from further up the time line. I know more now. I know it's strange, but time flows in all directions here sometimes. That's what I mean about being careful and having boundaries. You can get lost in your lost. But back to the past, and Fanna, and my training wheels.

The one thing you must realize is that your dreams are not all play. I am working most of the time. That's what I do. I'm one of those talented men and women who live exceptionally vivid dreams. We don't just float around in that other world, like 99.99% of all people do, catching a glimpse here and there of something so fantastic and different that sometimes it's terrifying, sometimes it's wonderful, and sometimes just cream & scream. It's a mission and someone has to do it. This is my story. Or rather, these are fragments of what happens in my sleep. Who knows, they may be hiring. If you have this talent, you too may be assigned to nocturne missions. Or you can enjoy hearing about some of my adventures, my drift, these night city blues (the theme of another story upstream).

So this perfectly manicured beach boy slides his tanned hand down my naked back, very sensuously, and my napkin flutters away, leaving me naked. From the look in his eyes, I looked mighty rumba just then. I sort of melted, or I let my will melt like a candle in his heat. He took me in both arms, and swung me around to the tune of, oh I don't know, what is that, a merengue or is it a more sensuous bossa nova or a samba or even some of that crazy Turkish pop. I find myself stepping along as if I had been doing this all my life. We are a team, he and I. Left, right, left right, turn, turn, left, right, left right, turn, turn…

I could do this forever.

But my new partner has other ideas. I can feel the hunger and the heat steaming from his chest.

There is vapor rising around our bare feet as we go step, step, turn, turn, left, left, right, right, back and forth, almost a tango with more bango…

I cannot stand any longer the swift glide of his palms up and down my bare skin.

My own heat is suffocating.

His hand finds its way, edge up, into the tenderness of my most private sex. My cunt is on the hunt. His cock is erect, and I reach for it with a trembling hand. I want to suck that thing and fuck it at the same time. Maybe in dreams you can do the impossible like that.

Having his cock and eating it too.

My center is on fire. My navel belches cannonades like a ship of the line. Every muscle in my body quivers with the rising heat, the tide, the first of several orgasms, each ripping me more until I am helpless.

His strong arms deliver me gently and gracefully onto my back and I only want to await his attack.

He descends on me, still dancing, and glides over me like a cloud casting its shadow. He's going to rain on my charade. I'm going to sprout like a flower. Oh god, am I wet. I reach up with both arms and pull him down. I am stronger than he thinks, and he is a little bird in my arms. Until he catches his equilibrium, slams my hands down on either side of my head, and stares me down like a cobra. He is the master, and I am just plaster. I hiss at him, pinned as I am on the grass. I am a serpent, wanting to be fucked. Take me if you are man enough. His eyes are like coals, his look fierce as a car's front grill coming at me ninety miles an hour.

I am too weak to raise my hands. They lie by my ears, while I toss my anguished face from side to side. The master slams one powerful hand under my left thigh and raises my leg. With his other hand and right knee, he opens me up to his assault. That cock comes at me like a war hammer. Its little hole is already wet from gunfire. We are both damp with longing, with yearning. I swear I am growing deaf with that Mediterranean music rumbling in the air.

I could have gone slow. I could have enjoyed a lot of sensuous necking. I would have liked to suck on him and make his cock so hard and tight that he doubled over. I would have enjoyed a real slowhand on my clitoris, making counter-clockwise circles like he knew what he was doing. He was racing too hard, and he took me with him. I was crying out for more before I even felt the massive thrust of his rod pushing me open. It is the moment when you are terrified that he will rip you. But I was so wet I must have been runny. Plus I sobbed with passion so that my bladder cried in powerless dribbles, like oil trickling out from a new find. Ramon--all men like this are named Ramon--lifted both my legs by heaving his hands under my knees. He pounded me so that my poor torso rippled with contractions and spasms. I wrapped my palms around his ass and tried to pull him tighter, but it was like reaching into a revving engine. It's lucky he didn't take my fingers off, the way that ass blurred. Looking over his shoulder, I could see the buttocks blurring in the air.

I grew weaker, slumped with my legs spread and knees pointing away from each other. That turned him on all the more. His movie star face, like one of those gigolos who prowl up and down some beach in Brazil, alternately doing tricks--eating knifes, swallowing fire--or winning martial arts bets with dark-skinned *sicarios*--or racing motorcycles, whatever--his handsome olive features showed a passion for me that made me want to take him home with me. I knew it would be like trying to tame a wild coyote. He thrust his tongue in my mouth. I felt his tongue hot and wet in one ear then the other. I felt his teeth nibbling at my nipples with gentle fury and downy intensity. He wanted my milk, and I wished I could spray him from my heart and soul. He sucked at me while I held first one tit, then the other, which ever he wanted, I was his servant, his slave, his girl, and I just wanted to please him so hard that I almost sobbed. I thrust my huge brown nipples at him. The sight drove him crazy. His eyes became wide and his mouth chuffed as if he were running miles. I begged him to take me, shake me, rake me, fuck me with that long steely shaft until, yes, he exploded in me. I could feel the gunshots. It was as if he'd been shot several times. Only he was doing the shooting. I yelled out loud for him to shoot me like that, rock me, blow it out and make me crazy, and so we came together. He spasmed, I spasmed. We yelled as we came together. We clung to each other like two drowning swimmers on a raft in a sea storm. We clung to each other for life, for sanity, for passion, with all the intensity in our cries and yells. I hugged him and pressed him to me like a baby when he collapsed on top of me. He was spent. He was limp. I reached down and fingered that mighty cock that now rested on my inner thigh, that soft wet place covered with his cum. I massaged it as if to say well done. Thank you. His little buttocks and those strong ass muscles were still hard as horn. I massaged him gently, and he sniffled appreciatively. He had it out of his system, and now we could go easy. I rubbed the head of his dick against my clitoris in contra-clockwise motions, enjoying the wet lube on my still throbbing little head down there. It was his head against mine. Two heads are better than one. Rubbing his glans against my hoodie made him perk up again. I could feel the steely cords in his powerful arms as he raised himself up to work toward the next orgasm. I felt myself grow, hard, my own hidden iceberg of joy radiating upward across my gut as the little nub stiffened with yearning. I cried out weakly as I felt him arch against me with new energy. Just that alone pushed me over the top again. He knelt between my legs and pushed his newly engorged yacht slowly up my boat channel. As I welcomed his force and size spreading me in our mutual wetness, I fanned my clit furiously and propelled myself to the I don't know how manyeth earthquake of spasms twitching me with joyful electricity. I felt a mighty cry rise from my gurgling throat.

And then I woke up.

Chapter 5. Interlude: On the Rocks with a Twist

The next moment (probably a day or two later, in the next dream), I was fully modest (even elegant) in a sugar dress with matching little vesty jacket (rounded corners, two walnut colored buttons) and a wonderful cream blouse with tiny red roses in full bloom. I sat beside Fanna at a bar. We were alone except for the bartender, an elderly man, sort of stout without being fat. He wore a merlot vest, white shirt, and black pants with suspenders dark blue as the last wink of evening in the tropics.

"Did you have fun?" Fanna asked. She used one strong hand (now caramel, not pale or blue) with glossy red nails to squeeze a twist of lemon around the rim of her Dubonnet glass. The rest of her (both of us, I saw in the mirrors) had a bluish-white glow in the bar light. She wore a loose-fitting, gathered skirt that generously extended down her long, crossed legs to mid-calf. Her upper torso peeked out in V-shapes from the black cottony top, with crossed halter straps looped over bare, bony shoulders.

Her arms were long and bare, smooth like caramel but tinged icy blue with reflections from the bar lights and mirrors.

While the bartender kept to himself, moving bottles, stirring ice cubes (rattling), wiping steel counters, we were alone after hours, it seemed. There were mirror walls behind the bar. The rest of the place was empty. Most tables had chairs upside down on them. Sliding glass doors, closed or locked, looked out over a great lawn under a half moon. In the distance loomed the million tiny checker lights of a city with great buildings wrapped in a bluish haze or marine layer while stars glittered peacefully high above. Distant piano music came from a lounge nearby. Plunk, plunk. Restful, contemplative. Time for bed, and I just got up. Or no, just fell asleep and here I am again.

"What happened?" I asked.

"You apparently woke up."

"Oh. And?"

She shrugged, sucking on her little green plastic drink stirrer. "How do I know? What happens in dreams stays in dreams. The opposite is true when we are awake."

"So my dream ended when I woke up for some reason."

"Yes, and in this state you don't know why. But you feel okay, don't you?" For an instant, she looked worried. She froze in the act of lifting a cocktail olive on a toothpick. Her ripe red lips stayed barely open.

"I'm feeling great."

She looked relieved. "Then it's working. The healing, I mean."

I fanned myself, thinking of Ramon. "Oh baby. Is it ever. Working, I mean."

She popped the olive in, made full-moompy mouth, and nodded as she tossed the toothpick basketball style into an ashtray a few feet down the bar. "*Mboob*," she said, which I translated as a happy *Good*.

"Is my name really Rosemary?"

She shrugged again. Olive gone, her mouth was clear to speak. "Is my name Fanna? What kind of name is that anyway?"

"Exotic."

"Like a parrot," she said with a crazy laugh. We were going to be giggly, I could see.

"You sound like a parrot," I said, and she took it with a good laugh. We were going to be friends, I could see. "Ramon fucks like a parrot."

"Is that his name? I thought it was José."

"Maybe you were with a different stud." I was guessing. She must enjoy it here too. Was she still healing? Whatever my problems in the real world were that required this much therapy--had she needed this just as much? I surmised that you really never get enough. Once you drink from these healing waters, your thirst never goes away. It just loses its desperation and dark yesterday. It's just here and now. For once, I am in a place where I don't need to look over my shoulder.

She shrugged. She was in a shrug Gish mood. Lightly so. "Let's talk about you. Are you getting what you need?"

I told her honestly after a moment's reflection: "It has been a long time since I didn't feel that sick dread in the well of my guts."

Her eyes flicked upward in recognition. "Oh yeah. That." She sipped her drink and made a happy face. "The twist is just right."

We clinked glasses.

I said: "Is there more?"

"Oh yeah. I'm just supposed to be with you-- interview you--between adventures to make sure you are on the right path."

"So, how old am I, Fanna?"

She shrugged. "I have no idea how old I am, much

less you. But they say you are as old as you feel. How old do you feel?"

I thought about my tearful, trembling entry into this wonderful world of calm and intrigue. "I'd say about thirty, maybe a little more. Not much more."

"Thirty three?"

I nodded.

She made that shoulder snuggle again, a shrug of acceptance. "That's what I figure. We have the sort of background energy of a young mother, I'd say, with a bastard in our life. I really don't know. I don't want to know. I'll deal with it on the other side. In here, Rosemary, we are free spirits."

We hunkered over our Debones, playing with our little lemon twists, while the bartender fussed over his glittering, starkly clean liquors and a wall clock ticked out a blurry image of something between about nine p.m. and midnight. We heard explosions of laughter and clapping from some distant party, maybe a magic show, or a strip tease--who knows? Who cares in here? I also caught the faint thunder of a passenger jet cruising among the light-squares of sky scrapers on its way to a landing. I heard the rush of distant highway traffic, or was it surf on a sandy beach under moonlight? This is such an amazing place or state of mind, whatever you want to call it.

"How did you find your way into this business?" I asked.

"I'll never know or care."

I regarded her for a moment. She seemed fortress-like, pent up. "It's a secret," I stated uncertainly.

She nodded. "So, Rosemary, I have to tell you." She found another toothpick, and stabbed it into the dark water of a little bowl of olives nearby. "I am told you are exceptionally talented for this."

"Meaning? Who says?"

"Management says. Meaning you have some of the

best espish qualities they have seen in a long time. Since me, in fact."

"Espish?"

"Yes, that's a general catch term meaning nothing specific, really, but it's Extra Sensory Perception." She added: "-ish."

I mulled that over. "Espish, eh? Learn something new every dream."

She chewed another olive, looking as if she was savoring every second. These are the green olives with bite, that have a little red pimiento slice in the heart where the stone was removed. I usually go for the sweeter, more nuanced dark olives with or without pits. I copied her, and stabbed myself a small handful of the olive-drabs floating in what looked like (but wasn't) sea water.

"We hope you will stay with us and go on missions for us later on, when you have mastered the program."

I drew a blank. "I don't see why not. Should I be cautious? Is there danger?"

She sat hunched over her drink, totally relaxed. I think she was relieved that I wasn't going to be a problem, despite my high energy and talent for this sort of thing. Not to mention (after Ramon) how I realized the extent of my passion. I was going to be a gourmet dreamer, the way some people indulge in exotic dishes cooked in weird tile kitchens with steel-framed lights and bare wooden trestle beams, you know, someplace like Berlin or Paris. No, make it a little more exotic--Brussels, or New Orleans, or maybe just to be different, Seoul. Like, add strangely pungent eel dishes or something, only we were not going to gain weight.

"Hey, Fanna."

"Yo, Rosie."

"Can I lose weight having sex in this place?"

She almost choked on her olive, breaking up laughing. "I never thought about it. Come to think of it, you can eat all you want here and not gain an ounce. But I haven't lost any weight, so the answer is probably no."

"Too bad."

"You look fine."

"I don't like my ass too much." I had not yet reached the point where I was happy with myself. It takes time, even in the dream world.

She waved a slender hand. "Don't worry. No matter what kind of ass you have, some guy will go nuts over it."

"You think? Only will it be a hot guy?"

She extended her forearms to either side, with her palms up and fingers wriggling as if she were checking for rain--or to see how dumb I am. "Is the Pope Catholic? Does a bear shit in the woods? Rosemary, you dope. You're a fine looking chick. And this is dreamland, remember? Here we look good and feel positive about ourselves. We're into sexual healing like the old Marvin Gaye song."

I remembered about him, and felt a little bad, but not enough to spoil my evening.

"Are you ready for another little adventure?"

"Yeah," I said, glad to take my mind off poor Marvin.

"You want to take a trip on the sexiest airliner in the world?"

"I'm game," I said, intrigued. What's the worst thing that can happen? *And then I woke up, right?*

"Ready?" Fanna said. She snapped her fingers in rhythm: "One, two, three."

Poof.

Chapter 6. Night Flight

What happens in my dreams stays in my dreams. I sat in the jet liner as it whispered over banks of clouds under a night sky filled with stars. I wore absolutely nothing, and felt a twinge of embarrassment, so I willed myself to be wearing a flimsy pink nightgown that came down to my ankles.

My dreams are mine.

I was having a dream. I think I had had an orgasm not long before, and I knew another one was coming (no pun intended) soon. I did not know where or when I was, and I did not care. I did not need to.

Nobody but me has any business knowing.

Outside, the moon floated like a white something, a face maybe or a headlight as of a car passing in the night.

My dream world is the only place where I am truly mistress.

Sitting in the dark, silent jet liner all around me were shadowy people. Most of them were asleep. Maybe some where ghosts. I didn't know or care. I was alive--that much

I knew, like so many things I knew and understood in my heart at that moment, without needing to be told. If there is such a thing as lucid dreaming, here we go.

My dreams are private.

My feet were bare, but I did not feel cold. I could feel hard, dry carpet under my heels and the balls of my feet. It felt good to rub my feet on the clean carpet, and feel electricity or heat or energy of some kind. As I felt this warmth, a nice comforter suddenly draped over me, dark blue like the edge of night. I was having such a good dream.

We need you, said the masked man.

A beautiful man with dark hair and a crisp coffee face leaned close from out of nowhere. He wore a steward's uniform--black coat, white shirt, skinny black tie. His name tag said Bonuit or Benoit or something French or French-Canadian. As he leaned close to speak with me, his breath smelled faintly like spearmint. His teeth shone even and white, and his dark eyes were set in china-white. A single thin stripe the color of merlot circled his dark sleeve behind just-visible white shirt cuffs. Matching braid graced his shoulder epaulets. The captain in the cockpit would have four such braids, the co-pilot three, and the chief cabin attendant (a tall, beautiful woman with a great lipsticked smile and glowing caramel skin who stood talking with another passenger far down the aisle) would have two such tokens of rank.

Will you serve us?

I learned about their ranks because, a while earlier, when the release-seatbelts lights quietly flashed, the chief came and sat beside me. She was a tall, elegant woman with strong hands and the most amazing deep-pink-almost-violet glossy perfect fingernails I had ever seen. She was tall and perfect, with a glossy *coiffure* the color of deep forest wood, brown as tree bark but faintly redolent of bubble gum or something girly and fun. She sat friendly, beside me in her dark uniform with two braids, hands folded in her lap in an authoritative but relaxed attitude. "How is your flight so far?"

Yes, I'll serve you, said I to the dark lady.

"Wonderful," I said. They had given me a small mocha pudding with tiny dark chocolate chips in it, to eat with a silver spoon from a glass ramekin, along with a steaming hot espresso, also in glass.

You will be rewarded beyond all your dreams.

"You won't remember anything," she said. "Our people saved you from an impossible situation.'

Let us begin then, said the master of clouds.

I had no idea what to say, so I shrugged and kept savoring my sweets. If something terrible had happened, I was ready to cry, but I didn't want to. I pushed the possibility away and imagined a memory of night, of peace, of a quiet bed in a quiet house in a quiet suburb (southern California, near the Pacific Ocean with its rolling breakers under full moonlight?).

No time to waste, said a dozen white-cloaked women in thickly falling rain.

"When you are ready, what needs will be revealed," said the woman. I could almost smell her fragrant, expensive lipstick. In a dreamlike state, I almost leaned forward and craned my neck to look closely at her beautiful teeth. I was such a child. I wanted to be like her. "You will learn what you need, and nothing more. You will be shielded at all times."

I'm as ready as I will ever be, I said with a sigh and lay back. Let the dreams begin. We were already in the air, reaching for cruising altitude. The engines were strong, the cabin quiet and dark, with just a few lights winking on and off in tiny red warnings. And that pretty much how my service with Nocturne Missions began...

"*Bruino* will attend to your needs," she said. She briefly brushed my knee with her heavy fingers. "Enjoy your flight. There is work ahead for you. Thanks for joining us, and we look forward to working with you." Her words were almost like a formal letter, and I half expected her to add a signature of some type (no pun intended; ha, I still had a sense of humor) but she rose and busily looked in half a dozen directions where she might be needed. What was the person's name? "*Briunff* (something) will be your attendant on this flight." I didn't catch his name, but it didn't matter. My own name was just a smear in the rain, a mixed up scramble of letters on a game board.

With that, and a blink of my eyes, almost a watery passage through tropical tides, she was gone. So was my pudding and so was my espresso but I'd had enough.

The same tall, dark, handsome young man stood beside me once again. He said in a slightly accented voice: "Do you wish for anything? Maybe a brandy, or tea? A pillow?"

I could still savor aftertastes of coffee and chocolate, and shook my head. The thought of a pillow entranced me, and I nodded happily, burrowing deeper into the warmth of my comforter. How did he know I wanted a pillow? I might have asked for brandy or tea, but I was too lazy. I just wanted to be toasty in my comforter, and a pillow seemed like just the perfect final touch. Or was it the perfect final touch?

Bonuit vanished for a twinkle and reappeared just as quickly with a small white pillow trimmed in lace. I had a hard time lifting my head, so he reached under the roundness at the back of my skull, under my thick dark hair, and gently lifted while with his other hand he pushed the pillow under my head. It smelled clean and linen and mommy. I moaned happily and folded my hands together under my cheek to sink into a deeper sleep.

It was my first such dream, on the way to Night City on a mission that had not yet been fully explained to me. I only needed to know (Need To Know, as such shadowy documents are very importantly stamped) that I should relax and everything would be explained later.

So I had a dream within a dream, in which I sat upright as we were all getting ready to deplane, as the expression among airliners goes. I had that wonderful sense of travel we have especially when we are young and single, and the whole world is new, and everything is an adventure. We are so lucky to live in this futuristic fantasy world where people fly around the atmosphere in these fabulous ships of the air, waited on by beautiful young men and women, and sipping drinks and munching on finger foods. We don't have a care in the world.

Sitting near me was a very elegant woman touching her lips and eyes with makeup. I wondered if she knew Fanna. She had pale, narrow features, a very red generous mouth, and large dark eyes under a wide, intelligent forehead on which well-defined, long thin brows made sensuous double bow. I was so jealous of her strong, noble features and the way she held herself. She must be a very important business executive or an actress in a major movie. She must be a billionaire, or is it billionairess? Or an heiress? Or both? How silly we babble in our dreams.

She seemed to hear me thinking, because she glanced toward me with sharp yet friendly eyes the color of warm, wet slate--gray, moody, impetuous. "Your dreams are your private world," she said for whatever reason. Nothing made sense, so why should that? I was all ears, as they say. I think the glow of my admiration must have shone on her. Was she embarrassed or was she used to it? Used to it, I think, because she was kind. She could not have been older than I was, however old (or young) that might be. With her authority, the way she carried herself, age was no matter. She might be thirty, or a thousand years of age. I think in our dreams we do not age.

"Did they take your baggage when you planed?" she

asked. I must have looked puzzled. She explained: "Planing is what you do when you get on the plane. Deplaning is when you get off."

I made an embarrassed little shrug, a curtsy, wrapped in grins, with my hands folded respectfully on my knees. I wore at that moment a dark-chocolate business suit, whose dress hem came to just above my knees. I seemed to have round, full knees, and pulled the hem down in embarrassment.

"You are too easily embarrassed," she said. She too, like the cabin attendant Benoit or Bonuit, had a faint accent of some European origin, but her English was flawlessly Midwestern U.S.A. without any regional peculiarities. "Don't be. Your dreams are your private country. You check your baggage when you plane. Did you hand everything over?"

I half nodded, half shrugged, seeming to remember only vaguely tipping a stout middle-aged man with a red cap--a sky cap, I guess they call them. "Yes, and I gave the sky cap a dollar for each bag, two bucks for the first one."

The lady nodded. "You are doing everything right. Relax, be comfortable, and enjoy your flight. You have a lot of work ahead of you."

"What exactly am I supposed to be doing here in my dreams?"

Her gunmetal blue eyes flashed haughtily. "We don't tell you until it's time for you to know. Everything is on a need to know basis."

"We?" I asked with a sudden sense of foreboding. She was my employer, my owner, my boss, my goddess, many layers up. I suddenly realized this, speaking of need to know. I needed to know, so she let me see the truth.

"I will be watching over you, so don't worry. You take care of me, and I'll take care of you."

"How do I do that?"

"Need to know. When the time comes, everything will be explained so your can accomplish your nocturnal mission in the city. It's really very enjoyable, with hints of joy and sadness and danger and exhilaration, like blues music."

"I see." I was perfectly satisfied with her explanation that wasn't an explanation so much as a down-boy or down-girl. "I will do everything I am told, to make you happy."

"I know," she said warmly. Somehow, it was as if she moved her warm hand full of blessings and hosannas over my poor little head, and rested her hand on my back for a moment. I felt filled with happiness and satisfaction. That is how it is in the dreams when you are on a mission. I'm not talking just ordinary raggedy ass dreams that people have where they are shivering and scared and crying for their mommy, or screaming as they fall out of fifty-story windows but wake up just before they go smack on the concrete. I understood that all people have good, busy mission dreams like these but most people are just tiny bit players in the great nocturnal drama of the night city blues and they never have any idea that we all live extra lives at night in our sleep. I had some special talents and that's why I was chosen for more important night work. At the same time, on that particular flight, I was still a young, raw newbie and had not a clue. That kind of made it all extra sweet and fresh and exciting.

My dream within a dream switched back to the outer dream, in which I was curled up on one side like a child, under my toasty quilt, with my hands folded under my cheek while Benoit or Bonuit was fussing over me.

"How are we doing here?" he said in a sweet, dark voice like forest honey that matched his five o'clock shadow (or whatever time the clock of facial hair reads).

"Mmm…" was all the noise I could make. I felt as if I had a huge marshmallow in my mouth, in a pleasurable kind of way.

"That's good," he said in a soothing tone, almost like a nurse bathing a patient. He took an extra long time about tucking me in, because I suppose it was a long night flight and that was really his job to make all of us passengers feel cozy and warm.

I became once again aware of Bonuit, standing over me as if he were frozen in time, slipping that pillow under my head, but I think he was tucking me gently in at the same time with big, dry, gentle hands. He had fingers like a pianist, like a musician, who knew how to strum my strings. He stood leaning over me, with both arms extended, fussing with the corners and edges of that soft, fluffy, airy quilt. He was a tall, muscular, wiry man with a narrow waist and a large shoe size. I could smell the warmth of that leather, and the cotton of his socks. He smelled nice, as if he'd just taken a shower with a very faintly fragrant, manly soap not long before. I made a mental note to ask him if he'd slept the night in a lovely, modern hotel in Paris or London, in L.A. or Montreal, or maybe someplace more exotic with palm trees and islander girls the night before planing. He had some s'planing to do.

"Can I get you anything else? A stuffed animal, maybe?"

As he leaned over me, I caught a gleam of his zipper and started salivating a bit.

Yes, I thought, eyeing his bulge. A stuffed animal would be perfect right about now. A toy goose with a long neck, or the swan that fucked Ledo in the myth of Zeus and the swan. Or was it Zeus and the Goose?

Getting goose bumps, I felt waves of desire pumping up from the well of, well, my well, for lack of a better term. Maybe those were memory waves of the earlier orgasm. Where had that been? Maybe in my bed at home in the waking (sleeping) world. In these dreams you remember little, usually nothing, so you have no idea if you are married or single, alone in bed or with someone, homeless in a ditch or lying in a mansion where every bedroom is as big as a city apartment.

Bonuit said nothing but made a cooing, approving noise, a little groan from the depths of his throat, of pleasure and approval, as my slender fingers with their faintly pink nail polish pulled down the hasp of his zipper. With my other hand still trapped as if glue between my cheek and the pillow, my free hand reached into the mysteries of his fly. My fingers fished around, familiarizing themselves. I felt warmth, and moisture. I felt hardness, soft around the stem but rigid as his desire complemented my feverish curiosity.

My hand found the trunk of his manhood and held it. He groaned. The stiffness was his desire for my touch. He wanted my lips there but in dreams we take our time. Everything flows at a different pace, like on a current in a stream glittering with moonlight. Only there was no glitter here. I had the quilt over my head, like a child in a tent, and nobody could see anything. As the lady said, my dreams are private. My dreams are the one place where I am completely in charge and there are no rules except what I want, and the limits I put on myself, only to stay out of danger if there is any. Flying is dangerous, let's face it. Dreams have their dangers, which is what makes them all the more exciting.

Fondling his Johnson, while he stood still over me, gripping the seat back behind my head with both hands. I needed for my hand to be wet, but my skin was as dry as his shaft. I sat up in the tent under my quilt so that both my hands were free. My dark, rich, full black hair hung down around me like a veil. I had become his island girl, and wanted to serve him while I took all that he had. I undid his belt, smelling fragrant leather. The gilded buckle twinkled and clinked faintly in the gloom under my quilt. I pulled apart the flaps of his trousers, finding white cotton shorts which I pulled down. I yanked them down with both hands, gripping the elastic band with my womanly paws. There it was, Mr. Glans, *sproinggg*, wobbling before me like a stiff tree in a breeze. It was big. I put my hands around it and pulled it to me, resting first one cheek against it and then the other. I puckered my lips and ran them up and down his shaft while he gave out a faint cry of surprise and pleasure. I felt one large, gentle hand kindly massaging my poor back while I devoted myself the worship of his crank. If our skin had been too dry--my hands, his saseech--I licked and kissed it up and down. It smelled faintly like the sea. There was also subtle coconut something, his soap on a rope probably in the shower, leaving a hint of tropical atmosphere in the hot box of his shorts. Hungrily, like a pig snuffling for truffles, my nose dug into the darkness and my lips sought whatever skin they could find amid the hard, crisp hairs. I held his balls in the palms of my hands and lifted them toward me, kissing them and licking them while his shaft stood straight up. Yes, he reached down and held it to give me access to the lower parts. Holding his manliness worshipfully, feeling their weight and fullness, I kissed my way up his throbbing mast (a long journey, taken slowly and with pleasure) until my lips fastened around the mushroom head and sucked, as if I were mouthing a lollypop.

At this, he held my head in both hands while he began to shake and quiver with growing passion. His large palms contained my face as if it were the most precious beautiful thing he had ever seen. At that moment, I am sure it was. I am pretty in a plain way, very pretty in a kind of scrubbed young way, and I was his goddess at that moment as he was carried helplessly on the current of his pleasure, the stream of his ecstasy, toward the thundering falls of his Niagara. He might have wanted to slip that slippery alligator in my mud, but he was too far gone by then. I put my hand between my thighs to form a tight knot for my muscles to squirm and turn around, fiery and flaming with their own need. I heard a great sob or a groan fly from my lips even as I pumped his head with my mouth as if it were a suction or a pussy or a hot vacuum perfectly fitted for what it was doing. I almost cried with desire, and could not get enough, as I swallowed the wads of spit and come that bubbled up inside, choking me. With both hands, I pressed against the hard wall of his steely abdomen, while his powerful hands gripped my skull, with my hair oozing through his fingers, as we both orgasmed at the same time.

In the next few moments, still shaking, he made folding motions as his body lost the stiff arc in which he'd strained above me. I felt his cock grow soft, though still thick and swollen, in my hands. My face was covered with sea sperm sprayed like rain on a bus window, and the tip of my tongue sought its salty jelly. He, meanwhile, sank to his knees as if worshiping me. He lowered his head between my legs. I let him do with me what he wanted. I still had orgasm left. My insides had just begun to quake with uncontrollable spasms. He pulled me toward him by the wideness of my ass, and lifted me like a cup to drink. He palmed the fullness of my thighs so that my feet bobbled helplessly in the air while he stuck his tongue in the runny slot of my heat. I could feel his tongue sliding through the shallows inside, poking into the hole of my fullness, and rising over the ammonia nostril of my pee maker, until it found the full, packed bundle of my clit. He knew exactly what to do, or I should say his tongue did. The tip of his tongue ran in slow circles around the fullness of my mound, which throbbed so that the shuddering traveled back into all deep regions of my body. My poor muscles twitched with electric current (was he an eel?) and my hands idly clawed the hair around his skull, holding without hurting, but firm. He moved with a certain rhythm, and my hands held his head and helped him piston through those gyrations as I melted. I opened to him and gave him everything while he treasured it with his tongue and held me like a chalice to drink from.

I was carried down that stream like a drowning woman. My hands sprang to my breasts, which were numb with exhaustion, but my nipples were on fire and demanded being sucked or fondled. I was able to pull first one, then the other, toward my mouth and encompass its swollen, tender purple in my lips. When I touched a nipple with my tongue, it was too tender to the touch, and recoiled with overload. Then I pulled that tit all the harder, sucking it as if to punish it, which gave me the final push to fall over the edge and have a long, sobbing, rhythmically rocking and shaking orgasm during which I might have squirted a little, so out of control was I.

I recoiled from his face, unable to stand a single volt or watt more of the power charge that had racked my body and shattered my quiet. I was spent, and collapsed inwardly with my soft, feminine legs draped over his hard, muscular, bony shoulders under that beautiful, one-braid uniform coat. His arms extended around me, encompassing the fullness of my feminine form in all of its firmness and softness while I enjoyed the strength of his cable-arms around me. Gently, I held his head against my belly, and stroked the fine hair on his head. I did not know him at all, yet I wanted him never to leave me. The way he clung to me, on his knees, and made faint mewling sounds of fulfillment, while his breath flared hot and passionate still between my soaked inner thighs, I had the sense he felt the same about me. I welcomed him in my arms as he rose up to kiss me, and I smelled the sea on his mouth even as I basked in the sunshine of his joy. I smiled like the moon with my eyes closed as I accepted him fully into my love.

In the layers and veils of dreams that rippled like curtains in a night breeze, I was once again sitting up and no Benoit or Bonuit in sight. Everything had suddenly changed, the way it happens a lot in dreams. The quilt was gone. I wore that chocolate suit again, with nylon hose (caramel) to match, and fine leather pumps that smelled of a shoe store still. I was relaxed and calm, I was dry and composed, I was not wet with come or pee, in fact I was very lady-like and fully dressed. Opposite me once again sat the elegant woman, my boss, my owner, my whatever the fuck, I was glad and fully accepted being a pup in this strange world. She held up a compact and dabbed her wide, generous mouth with one last, glossy red lipstick dot before tossing the gold cylinder in a small hand purse at her side. She wore a gray business suit with a pleated skirt of some dim autumn pattern and a little jacket with rounded corners and small, rumply wool lapels. Her hair was dark red, like autumn apples, only a little darker like evening. Her hair was full, and wavy rather than curly, cut in bouncing bobs that flew left and right with the motions of her fine head on a slender neck.

She sat across the aisle on my left, one row ahead of mine, so that she had to turn to speak with me, but she only glanced at me sidelong. There was kindness in her eyes, but I wasn't important enough for the full body language of turning to face me. So I leaned as far forward as I could (suddenly I was wearing a seatbelt, and the no sex sign flashed, or was it no smoking, or were those the same thing?) while she half turned her head to speak to me. "You will have classes shortly and learn what you need to know."

I was pleased with the dream world so far, still throbbing and full of embers and trembles from my orgasm with Bonuit, and I had no complaints. I wondered if I would wake up at any time soon. She seemed to read my mind. "Your dreams are of a different time flow than in your waking life. When you are here, you do not remember your waking life, and when you are awake, you have no idea that you spent hours or even days in the dream world. That is how this works. Think of it this way. We spend a third of our lives sleeping. If you live to be ninety, you have slept for thirty years or more. Surely you don't think nature wastes that time or that nothing happens, do you? You are one of the rare, talented ones like I am. One day (or night) maybe you can be a suit like me. Until then, enjoy being a gofer and a newbie."

"Oh, I am enjoying it very much," I said. I kept my hands politely folded together on my seat rest. "Where did my new friend go?"

She smiled slightly. "You like each other. That's nice. He will be back soon. You take care of each other, hear?"

As she spoke, the jet liner changed engine pitch and began tilting slightly to land. A vast flood of lights visible below must be the night city whose blues I was going to sample. The full moon hung like a girl's pimply face amid the veil of faint stars. I felt myself falling into a deeper sleep. Maybe I snored a bit. I woke up, feeling parched, and padded to the kitchen to get a drink of water, but that was all vague background music. I was in a dark, safe place I called home. I was not alone, but I had no idea who my loved ones were, nor was I supposed to know. On these nocturnal missions, you go through a membrane, a force, that lets you in and out, but does not let you take your memories with you.

What happens in your dreams, stays in your dreams.

I was padding around in bare feet in a dream place, not my home. Let the dreams roll on, I thought. I went back to bed, curled up, and woke up back on the airliner. The cabin was just like before. Passengers were settling in to sleep. I looked around for my new friend, Benoit--but I am afraid it was Bonne Nuit, Good Night. I settled contentedly with my head against the porthole, looking out over passing fields of city light far below. I vaguely felt a stewardess' hands tucking me in. A fresh little pillow with a crisp coverlet smelling of starch and steam got lightly whacked into the space between my hair and the window. A light but surprisingly warm blanket found its way over my pulled up knees and gathering dream bubbles. I wondered, while passing out, if you could have a dream within a dream, because this certainly felt like I was going deeper and deeper, layers down...

Chapter 7. Special Talent

Wow, you are good," Fanna said. We were walking on the beach someplace sunny, with flawless blue skies, not a single shred of cloud in them. Surf curled in with the rhythmic growl of someone snoring (speaking of sleep, if we must). Gulls shot by, cawing nastily. Not everything in dreams is lovely. Some of it is downright realistic, including the sea gulls fighting over one another's kills in the shallow water where foam slips in and out with the tide. People in bathing suits sat on towels, looking out to sea with great big sunglasses for eyes, under assorted hats. The air smelled of sea weed, sun tan oil, fish sandwiches, and gasoline. That's civilization for you. Our dreams can be quite real, capturing what is good, bad, ugly, and nice. Or was I getting better at this dream walking stuff?

I was still trying to catch my breath. "Where did he go?"

"You fell asleep."

"In the middle of sex? That's what a man would do."

"Don't be hard on men."

"Hard on, men?" We both laughed. "So I passed out?"

"It happens."

"I think I had an orgasm before I faded."

"That's usually how it goes. Well, you did it. At least you didn't wake up this time."

"Again." I was disappointed. "I can't win."

"Now, now, the night is young."

Fanna and I both wore bikinis. Hers was pink, with a cute little stringy bow on each hip. I guess the suggestion was that her dream man could pull one of the bows, and her privacy would come apart. She wore a mannish, long-sleeved white dress shirt over that, with a pattern of fine coffee colored pattern stripes running the long ways, like from wrist to shoulder, from bottom hem to button-down collar. She looked really stunning, under a wide-brimmed straw sun hat with a pink silk band that was too wide and cute to be a man's. What else? We both wore black nylon deck shoes (with fine, almost neon blue trim) that you could rinse in the surf after you inevitably got sand in them, especially between your toes. She was pretty much looking pink today, even her light lipstick. She was not the wintery fae who had first brought me through the airlock from my nasty memories to my new, unburdened state of paradise.

I tend to go for black, as was the case with my bikini. No strings, no suggestions. I wore a light yellow custard blouse without ornament, although I did wear a lovely coral necklace with a large heirloom cameo between my collar bones. I wore a dark blue baseball cap, with my hair in a pony tail that flounced through the snap in back, the way women signal (at least I think) that they are sporty. Like I am up for anything. I will outrun you, out-climb you, out-swim you, and out-think you. Of course that's what they say bears in the wild will do to a human. I hardly have the fur for it.

We carried rolled up towels and beachy hand bags-- mine cream stripes with blue sea shell and orangy starfish motifs, hers black and white checkered with (yes) pink Las Vegas themes like dice and cards. We found a nice spot along the half mile mark, halfway between the old Victorian hotel at one end and a seaside golf course at the other. It felt good to plop down on the hot sand, with clean beach towels under us, and just do nothing. Of course, we talked.

I asked: "Do people often dream of sitting on the beach?"

Fanna seems to shrug a lot when I ask questions. I think it means I ask too many questions and she really doesn't give a squat about the answers. I never learn. She said: "All I know is that shrinks and fortune tellers and all those sorts of people seem to think that everything in a dream has some symbolic meaning."

My rejoinder was: "If they make their money explaining dreams, I guess they have to come up with some mystical malarkey for every moment."

"Whatever suits the occasion," Fanna said.

We sat for some minutes, leaning back on our palms, and starting at the sea. We must have looked like almost matching book ends. I think our heads probably turned in unison every time some studly young hotel employee chuffed past, bringing lunch to couples sitting in Hotel De Javu beach chairs or on Hotel De Javu towels. Not to mention HDJ beach umbrellas. The Hotel De Javu had the whole operation locked up, including the golf course. A group of cute young men (and a few tanned, athletic looking girls in baseball caps with flouncy pony tails as I just described) would regularly ride back and forth on golf carts between the hotel and the golf course a mile up the beach. On the cart they carried people (tourists, by their strange clothes, cameras, and amazed looks); golf clubs;

or pizzas and the like. We laughed when one young man drove past on a HDJ golf cart with a huge English sheep dog sitting on the back. I could swear the dog (though you couldn't see its face for all the fog of hair) was laughing out loud with his tongue hanging out. Why should he go charging around on the hot sand like a fool, maybe chasing a Frisbee, just because some humans said so.

"I wonder if he is having a dream too," I remarked.

"That's hilarious," Fanna said. "Looking for a female."

"Fifi."

"Yeah. A poodle with pink bows on her collar. They'll run in circles sniffing each other's holes."

"Like people do, only maybe a little more subtly."

"Like how subtly," Fanna said, staring in the direction of a couple of young Guidos with their shirts open to their belt buckles, with gold medallions visible. They strutted along the water, rocking from side to side, with powerful arms that reached to their knees. Probably football players. Big game in town at the stadium, my dream memory told me. Each had his chest exposed ready to pound his fists on and yell *Ahh-HOO-Ahh, HOO-ah, HOO-ahhhh* like Tarzan, *Yodel-ee-doo*. Their sunglasses could not hide the hunger and aggression in their eyes as they stared after every piece of bikini bottom.

Fanna looked at me suddenly. "Wanna?"

"Nah," I said. "I'm just now not in the mood for Italian. Maybe later."

"I didn't mean pizza," Fanna said.

"No pepperoni today."

She laughed. "That's so cheesy."

"Slice of life."

She poked her finger in her throat and made retching motions. "Twenty thousand comedians out of work, and they had to hire you."

I gave up on life and lay back on the sand. I wished

we had an umbrella. The sun sizzled us. We smelled like bacon broiling away in a marinade of SPF-50. Kind of a nice coconut-banana aroma, come to think of it. "I don't have the energy to fuck, or even look," I told Fanna.

"Me neither." She copied me. She lay back, with her hands folded over her bare navel, and pulled her straw hat down over her eyes.

After a few minutes she said: "Would you be up for a real mission?"

"You mean, a nocturnal emission?"

"Yes, sort of, if it comes to that."

"Comes?"

"Oh jeez, I am going to run away from you."

"I am definitely interested. What kind of mission?"

"Snow globing. Give it a shot. The folks who review our progress--"

"--which is who?--"

"I don't know," she said.

"Give me a break."

"No really. It's outside the dream. Nothing passes through the membrane of stupor. What happens in your dreams stays in your dreams."

"Fair enough. So how do they communicate with you?"

"Through my thoughts."

"Telepathy." I must have grown up Italian because I ask a question by making a statement in an ironic tone. It's a nice talent. I can also make saseech fingers in your face, raise my chin like a weapon, and exclaim "Ey! Oh!" So I have a clue about my real life. And I know there is an old Calabrian saying: "A wife needs a good beating every week or two." Of course, it happens, but you have to *capisc'* (cabbeesh) the irony in the tone. Seeing those two guys with their dark, curly hair sent me a clue about myself. I made a face of stone when they looked in my direction. For a pair of stud bucks, they turned pale and looked away. No eye contact with this virago.

"Yeah," Fanna said, "telepathy, I guess. Ever since I became a Guide and a Helper, they'd laid this psychic pipeline to my door. I don't even know who They is. One of them was my Guide long ago when I came through the keyhole bawling and trembling like you did, poor thing."

I was amazed. "That seems like so long ago."

"It's been a week or two."

"No."

"Yeah. You learn fast. You're good at this. And--"

"--Yes--?"

"They noticed you have a cool weapon."

"Me?" I was genuinely amazed and caught off guard. "What do I have?"

"That hand."

"Okay, I'm without clue number uno."

She rolled over on one side and looked at me with a wry expression. "You remember the guy in your dream? Benoit?"

"Boner."

"That guy." She grinned. "The way you unzipped him and slid your hand in…it was smooth as classical flute."

I thought back, and only remembered being in a red haze of arousal. Yes, I had slid his zipper down.

"You unzipped him before he had any idea. You reached in like a pickpocket, without his knowing it, and grabbed his cock."

"Ah yes. It's all coming back to me now." I could remember the heft of his Louisville Slugger in my paw.

Fanna said: "Someone once told me--a very wise lady of some experience in these things--that men are like wild animals. They are almost impossible to capture and tame. She did say, however, that as long as you have a man's cock in your hand, he is helpless. It's like throwing a turtle on its back, or whatever the urban myth is, and the turtle can't move. It's like that with a man. If you can get your hands on his cock--to say nothing of your lips around it--he is putty in your hands."

I laughed. That did seem to have a ring of truth about it.

She laughed too. "I watched you."

"You watched me?" I was outraged.

She nodded. "The folks at the Institute, who have harnessed this espish talent for healing purposes, carefully observe their patients. Our patients, since I am now Staff. You have a rare talent. In a man, it would be called balls. In a woman, I supposed you'd call it tits. You have the tits to unzip a guy, slide your hand in there stealth-combat before he knows anything. He's still talking you up, bullshitting and telling you whatever he thinks you want to hear so he can maybe dream about getting up your skirt within a day or two--and you have already pounced. He's still talking, and you already have his cock in your mouth and you are sucking like it's one of those grape popsicles we used to get as kids on hot summer days."

I laughed. "Benoit did sort of taste a bit like grape flavor."

"You bad girl."

"Oh, I was very good."

"Yes you were."

We gloated together at how good it is to be bad. Not the other way around. All our lives, authority figures have been telling us that it's bad to be good or feel good. Today's dream girl flips them on their heads. It's great to be bad.

"So as long as you have his raw in your paw, you own him," Fanna said of the generic, cosmic male. "We like that, and think you may be ready for a little preliminary test mission, just to get your interest and hopefully keep you in the game. It gets better all the time."

I considered. "Yes. Well, um, as you say, what's the worst that can happen?"

"You can wake up," Fanna said.

"I can fall out of bed and break my leg."

"You have too much imagination."

"No, paranoia. I could be having sex in a dream, whaling away and wailing as I head for climax, and suddenly fall out of bed, break my neck, and die."

Fanna's jaw dropped. It took her a moment to choke back her laughter. "You are insane. I don't know you."

"Just saying."

"Paranoid."

"You have to consider every angle."

She said: "Look at it this way. You could walk out the door one morning and get run over by the ice cream truck to the tune of Pop Goes The Weasel. Live a little, Rosemary. That's a big part of why we are here. You are so uptight. And you have that razor-sharp sarcastic attitude that makes you so adorable."

"Oh thanks. Well, Benoit went for it, as did Ramon. I'm two for two."

"I think his name was *Bon Nuit*, which means Good Night." She shook her head lightly, staring at me, and collapsed back on her towel.

I wasn't sure if she'd lost consciousness. "Yes," I said.

She looked as if she'd had general anesthesia.

"Yes," I repeated.

"Yes what?" she mumbled.

"I'll do it. I'll try one of those nocturnal emissions."

"You are too punny for words. Shut up for a while. I want to rest."

"When do we start?"

She had her hands lazily slapped together over her belly. Without opening her eyes, she murmured: "Patience is a virtue. Relax and rest. Remember, you are probably at home, asleep in your bed. You need your beauty sleep. All in good time."

But you know--a moment later was a night or two

later, and I was in the next dream. That's how seamlessly these things sometimes blend together at the edges. Especially in the hands of a great Guide like Fanna. No matter how I teased her, she gave back in kind. It is very strong, this juju sleep thing.

There came a point when I started to ask more questions. As I became more sure of myself, and more comfy with who I am, I started asking: Is there more? Is this all there is?

Fanna's response was: "There is more to do than you can imagine. There are more people to help than either of us could in a lifetime."

"And mostly it's about having sex with them?"

"You are sometimes such a child," Fanna said. "Sexuality is part of our persona as human beings. We are wrapped in an aura of sensual, passionate desire every moment of our adult lives--past puberty. Until we are mature, we are off limits like candy until we reach that certain age like when we can drive a car, drink in a bar, and serve in the military. That sort of thing. But to your point, Rosemary, it's about helping others to reach fulfillment in their dreaming souls. The scientists at CTI believe that it's in dreams where we encounter the problems we could not solve while awake. Because society makes us so repressed, we shy away from our passionate, hungry, needy inner woman (or man, since the same thing applies to the other gender)."

"What about gay men, lesbians, transgender, bisexuals, other?"

"Gender is a reference like saying someone is black or white. There are no black people, and there are no white people--just a thousand shades of melanin in the skin, and some evolved differences in some body features like lips, nose, and the like. As any surgeon will tell you, we are the same under the skin. Same thing applies to gender. There are no straight people or gay people or whatever handle you use. There is a spectrum, and everyone's kink is somewhere on that grade. It's just another of the many anxieties we fight with in our subconscious lives, which we can see and exercise here in our dreams."

I paused to think about it, and felt very warm and accepting of everyone as long as they didn't hurt others (or themselves). That's the key here--not hurting yourself, or letting others hurt you. It's all attitude, remember. I happen to be a woman strongly interested in men. I have no interest in women sexually. I just had this warm, wooshy, balmy sensation, almost like a very faint but shuddering orgasm, that I really didn't care what I did with whom, as long as we loved each other in that moment of passion. I mean, love, as in caring and wanting just the absolute joy for the other person, not marry joy or romantic let's run away together type of thing.

Chapter 8. Dreams Within Dreams: Surfer Girl

I learned a surprising thing too. That it's possible to have dreams within dreams. I faded on Fanna at that point. I found myself in an armchair in some unknown, fuzzy, foggy place in the dream world, and straddling my lap was an attractive young woman wearing a miniskirt, a summer blouse, and a pink band in her blonde page boy hair. Her full thighs rested on my thighs, and her vanilla calves were tight against mine. She had blue eyes, a kind of boyish surfer face but totally feminine, and she was just sprawled on me. My arms were wrapped around her waist, and I could feel the rising and falling of her breaths (rapid). Her mouth was parted near mine, and I heard her breathing (breathy). We were grooving at the warmth and softness of one another's bodies. Her weight on me was like a blanket, and a tight one at that whose pressure contained me and made me feel warm and throbby.

I had no idea who she was, or where that came from, or where it was going. I kind of wish I knew more, but then I'm sort of glad I let it be what it was.

We throbbed together and had a low, purring orgasm of happiness. I remember her bare arms were flung over my shoulders, and she buried her cheek against the throbbing artery in my neck as we made cooing, dove noises together. Warmth rose out of my belly like birds flying out of a cage. I was wet down below, as if warmth were flowing down the insides of my thighs.

The moment and the vision were over before I could catch my breath. That was a dream within dreams, possible only in the dream world. And then I woke up, you might say, except there I was still in dreams and so contented.

I did ask Fanna about it, some time later, over drinks on the beach in Coronado. She told me: "That can happen. She was probably someone who was attracted to you in her own dream world. Maybe that chair was in her place, who knows where."

"So she threw herself on me?" I remembered the good feeling, and at the same time wasn't sure I wanted to ever have it happen again--maybe with a twenty something man, like a baseball player or surfer, same everything, but a hard package between my legs. I almost got wet again, thinking about it. Whatever that was, it was somehow mutual between me and blondie. I could remember the wide, soft feel of her behind in my palms, and felt a mixture of squeamish and dreamish.

"What happened was mostly in her dreams--so says my experience," Fanna said. "She must be a powerful espish in her own right. But you know--don't worry about it. You know what I read into it? That she must be extremely needy, and very loving, and she gave you a good throbbing. Just look at it that way, and let go. Move on."

Chapter 9. Dancing at the Hotel De Javu

W elcome back," said Fanna. We were on the beach (still, or again, maybe a day or two later) and she was just standing near me, shaking sand from her beach towel.

I blinked a few times, unsure of what had just happened. I remembered the blondie experience with detached pleasure. It was so yesterday already. I felt some inhibition and started gathering courage to ask Fanna about it. We were going to have that moment on the beach outside the Hotel De Javu later tonight. There was yet a tiny moment left in that dream within a dream. But I'll get to that shortly.

After a moment, I realized it was dusk. The sun was setting like a spattered egg yolk amid scrambled orange clouds intertwined with a grayish, pearly marine layer. The air smelled of kelp and salt, and the screaming gulls had gone to their motels for the night, or wherever sea gulls go to rest from their yelling and fighting all day.

When you have meetings in dreams, as I was to learn,

they can happen anywhere--both the dreams and the meetings, I mean.

It's not like the waking world, where you meet with your doctor at a hospital, or you meet with your shaman at a place of worship, or you meet your spouse for lunch at a pricey restaurant. You get my drift.

You could end up meeting on a mountain top seven miles above sea level--and not need oxygen tanks. Thanks, but no tanks.

I was getting used to my sexual garden, this paradise of abandon and delight, so it did not surprise me when Fanna invited me to a rooftop meeting with her supervisor, Dr. Joseph Street. It was a moment of interest to me especially because this was my first purposeful meeting with a man in my dream world. To date, I had been closely monitored by Fanna, who has become my best friend in the world (awake or asleep, I think, though of course you never really know what's going on in the other half of your life, meaning when you stumble out of bed, brush your teeth, and are subject to the everyday laws of wakeful reality).

Fanna looked just as she had a day or two earlier in my previous dream. I was smart enough by now to realize that dreams can continue almost seamlessly, depending on circumstances--some under one's control, most not so.

"We meet again," Fanna said. "Hurry, Rosemary, and pack up your stuff. We're going to the hotel to meet Joe Brindletail. You'll like him."

"I must have gone on with my life," I said. It's funny how you don't feel tired in dreams, even if it seems you are running marathons. In reality--correct that: in dreams-- we must have been here on the sand for several days. I was just picking up where we left off longer than you can hold your breath.

There was a little chill in the air. Fog began rolling in across the Pacific Ocean or whatever its equivalent was here on De Javu Island, outside the Night City. I wondered if Night City became Day City when it was light out, but decided probably not, because most people are home in bed sleeping. Actually, most people have very little psychic muscle and low batteries, and no clue about how to manipulated and control their dreams. As Fanna had explained so logically, we are filled with dreams. Think about it. I thought about it as we strolled (at a purposeful pace) along the hard-packed, wet sand beside the darkening surf. The last glow was on the ocean horizon. A full silver moon rose, and cast its cold light on the roiling waters in my dream world.

Think about it. We live in a moment. The present is a fleeting shred of time. Living is really like riding a bicycle on a sixteen-lane freeway. You have trucks and cars and busses whizzing around you in both directions. You are pedaling as best you can on your rusting old Schwinn. Occasionally, a tractor-trailer air horn blares at you. You can only respond by tooting that plastic horn with the rubber squeeze-bubble screwed to your handlebars. *Toot!*

Every moment, the universe flies past you. Every moment joins the past before you can go *Toot* on your handlebar horn. The future does not exist yet. That's all the cars five minutes or five hours up the road yet in both directions, that will soon rush past you into the oblivious past. Where you are, pedaling desperately, is the present. In front of you are the *nothing* and the *not yet*. Even on your bicycle, you leave each granular atom of *now* behind and ride into the next moment, and the next, and the next, without end. The only differences between the future and the past are that (a) you can see the past in your memories, whereas the future is invisible; and (b) the future has yet to come, while the past can never come again.

Now add to that the fact that we ride along, most of us, burdened by guilt, fear, and other negative thoughts and energies. We carry over our back a giant sack of memories. If you are like me, like a lot of us, that bag has more bad memories than good ones. Yet we continue to shlepp that dreck around with us. It's like never getting around to cleaning out the garage, which is typically jammed to the ceiling with 'good stuff' we must never get hauled away to the dump. When we die, the next home owner does hire a guy with a big truck to come and take all that 'good stuff' to the dump anyway.

That is why we come to the dream world. We come here because it frees us of that giant bag of useless stuff that is often not just worthless but actually toxic and deadly. Here in the dream world, you become free of all that junk.

It's all so strange but that's the reality of our universe. So trust me--the dream world is logical. It makes as much sense as anything else in this fleeting dream where (as in the traditional song of English aristocracy being rowed on picturesque rivers, as in "row, row, row your boat, merrily down the stream" (and why would you need to row if the river is already carrying you down stream? See what I mean? It's like riding that bicycle on the freeway.) "merrily, merrily, merrily, life is but a dream."

Good luck.

Toot!

Chapter 10. Snow Globing: Missions & Adventures Yet To Come

That's actually the kind of stuff Fanna and I talked about as we strolled to the Hotel De Javu, which rose out of the sand like a white fairy castle with red roofs, including round and square turrets. From each turret fluttered a pennant, and from the largest fluttered a majestic flag.

"Doctor Street invited us to meet him at the corporate headquarters downtown," Fanna told me. "You'll find him very interesting."

"Is he a medical doctor?"

"No, he is an assassin. Or he was, until he became operations chief of the Clandestine Branch of the Second Service. That's espionage. They steal secrets from other countries or from large corporations. Sometimes they kill people. They also have a huge database of really good recipes. He also goes by the name Joe Brindletail sometimes."

"They kill people in dreams? I thought that couldn't

happen?"

"They wish them away," Fanna explained. "Maybe they wake up wherever they are sleeping, and can't get back to sleep. Insomnia. That's the weapon of assassination in the dream world. You can't dream if you can't sleep. You can't really kill someone in a dream, so it's more like wishing them gone."

"Lots of coffee," I said. "We could develop a coffee weapon that flies around the world and falls on your enemy, making them wake up and disappear from dreams."

"Not so quick, Rosemary. I've heard ghost stories. Like about the Hotel De Javu. There is a beautiful young woman who lurks there, or her ghost does. She died a mysterious and violent death on the back stairs over a century ago, on the night of a terrible sea storm that covered the noise of the gunshot. Nobody knows for sure if she was murdered, or if she killed herself. She should be gone from the hotel, but a hundred years later, people still report finding her in bed with them, fully clothed, lying there awake and staring at the ceiling at three a.m."

I felt a shudder. "Oh my god. That would scare me to death--finding a strange person lying in bed with me."

"They say she's clutching an umbrella, and wears a hat with an ostrich plume in it. Imagine if she finishes your plate for you at breakfast as you happen to glance out to sea. Or she's the extra guest in the taxi, who never got in and never got out and never said a word to anyone, but everyone thought she was just someone who belonged there."

"Do they have eye contact?" I was prepared to scream.

"Sometimes."

Eeeeeeekkk!

"Rosemary, cover your mouth when you scream. You didn't brush your teeth before you went to bed. And you must have had garlic and onions for dinner."

About that last moment from my blondie dream now. Fanna and I got ourselves drinks at this wonderful pub looking bar. Everything inside the Hotel De Javu is old wood, like a sailing ship but done up in mahogany and lacquer so the surfaces glow. The lighting inside is soft and yellowish, amber in places, or the occasional dim green exit light thing. The place smells of some soft bubblegum carpet cleaner. There are always young people in housekeeping uniforms bustling about vacuuming or dusting or carrying trays or bags. They wear black bottoms (skirt or pants) and white blouse, red vest, black flat shoes, the women with black hose under their kneetop skirts, the men's trouser legs hemmed the old fashioned way. Bell hops in red pill box caps occasionally trawl by in blue-on-khaki uniforms. All the different services have slightly different uniforms. Guests mill about looking like tourists anywhere, except these are dream trippers (and dream tippers, as they slip virtual bills or coins to contented looking staffies).

"We'll meet Dr. Street in the Elephant Bar," Fanna told me. We found a corner with plush chairs. The light came from cut and brushed glass wall sconces. The wallpaper was Victorian, over wainscoting of dark wooden slats. The carpets were plush plum and vaguely what used to be called Oriental, while the chairs were a rouge velour on dark square legs. Every little set of three or four chairs centered around a round coffee table of dark wood with a wheat or white stitched, round doily on it.

As guests milled about, we sat in the quiet of our corner. Across the room, under amber sconce light, a party of two distinguished looking, middle-aged men and their (presumably) matching wives like aging peacocks took seats. One or two staff swooped in to take orders, to clean tables--and I saw my blondie.

She was the ghost from my sensuous dream. This

was no long-ago mysterious stranger, but a modern woman with her own intriguing world. She was a cute young surfer, in that boxy, business-like, flat-footed Anglostuffy sort of outfit--black shoes, sheer dark hose over firm calves and strong thighs under swinging, demure over the knee black dress. She wore a white apron, white blouse, dark crimson vest, and black cutie bowtie (feminine). She had that sharply handsome athletic face (feminine, soft), with hungry blue eyes that raked me for a glowing instant like coals of starvation and (embarrassed honesty, longing?) before I blinked and she whooshed away on her duties, never to return.

Fanna caught the transaction and said cryptically: "So you learn something more. Time flows differently here in dreams. She just saw you for the first time, and wanted to throw herself on you. Instead she appeared in your dreams days ago. You'll probably never see her again. She's cute."

"She'll find some guy."

"Or girl."

We sat quietly nursing our drinks in the corner of the Elephant Bar annex while people came and went. It's always nice to people watch. You see all the little dramas.

Before I could get too deeply into that reverie, a nice looking man approached at a quick clip. He was tall, dark, and handsome, wearing an almost dark-silvery, rich business suit, very light cranberry shirt, and dark red necktie with a gold clasp. On the tie clasp was a black oval (onyx?) with the letters inset in fine gold (art deco script): CTI. "I'm Joe Steel," he said. "So sorry to keep you waiting." He rushed up to us with one hand extended. Like many tall men, he bowed forward to reach down to us. Fanna smiled familiarly and shook hands. I felt sort of blank as I held his firm, dry hand briefly. It was like holding a sheaf of bank notes. He had this feeling of power about him that made my insides flutter. What got me most was his eyes. He had cold, almost hard sort of dark green eyes the color of moss, but for an instant, they seemed to crack or bend or something. For that instant, he regarded me with personal uncertainty. I think he found me attractive. I dared not believe this. I got the feeling he was surprised that I was more (something?) than he had expected. "Rosemary," he said. "Miss Evening."

"Is that my name?"

"Yes. In the dream world, that is your name. We chose it for you." He recovered from his imbalance, almost over-compensating as he sat down with a tug on his crisply ironed gray suit trousers. He wore form-fitting elastic night-blue socks, and black almost pointy shoes so shiny I blinked several times. His rounded toe pieces caught the drunken amber light and made me feel hypnotically weary. He had that much power--very espish, much more than my fledgling talent.

"Chose?" I spoke as if I had been drinking too much thick, syrupy brandy. My tongue and my lips seemed swollen or glued together or something.

He looked sharply at Fanna. "Is she in there for us?"

Fanna nodded. "She is totally here tonight. Deep in the dream world, like you and I."

He regarded me. "Hello, Rosemary. So nice to meet you at last."

"Nice to meet you," I said through a fog. I pushed my drink away.

"I'm sorry," he said with a crisp little smile amid beard shadow. He had small, beautiful teeth. "I am probably coming on a bit too strong. I'll throttle back."

Fanna chortled, a sound from her long, elegant neck. She was pretty. "You're making me break a sweat, Joseph."

Evidently, she and Joseph had some history. I am not wall-flowerish about these things. Especially by then I was getting my sea legs (or dream legs?) so to speak. He noticed.

"You are becoming more sure of yourself," he said. His face was narrow and smooth--easy on the eyes, as the expression goes. His dark eyes glittered sympathetically, though there was something dangerous and thrilling about him. He wore his black hair smoothly combed, with a full part on the left side, and a gorgeous, glittery wave running down to his forehead and back up, over his right ear. He was maybe upper thirties, without any gray showing. His complexion was smooth, with a hint toward olivine (Mediterranean).

"Is your name really Street?" I asked in a sassy tone as the drunken hypnosis lifted.

He smiled his best Godfather Junior grin. "Actually, it's Antonio Viale. You are perceptive."

"You are Italian."

His black eyebrows furrowed in puzzlement. "Yes, and I'd have to review your file. Are you Italian?"

"I have no idea." The words just bubbled up from me, sassy as hell. "I hope so. I think my soul must be Sicilian. I get nervous, I start dancing the Tarantella, poison spider dance."

"Oh, from the tarantula," he said faintly, knowing the background. He eyed Fanna as if to say This tiger is on the loose from her cage; which was not a bad thing, because it was clear he wanted me to be strong. I was going to say he eyeballed her, but that would imply what I suspected-- namely that he had balled her sometime in the past, being a ladies' man. And what man in his right nut would not want to eye Fanna and ball her? I could tell from the pleased, flushed look about her, and the smug, self-assured conquest in his look. I wouldn't mind his assaulting my castle, honestly. For a moment I felt like a giant bunny, regarding him with a hilarious look, while I imagined I was about to chomp on the gigantic carrot hanging between his knees.

He regarded me, looking puzzled at the hilarity in my

gaze: "You are still getting used to this, Rosemary. I have excellent reports on your progress."

I looked at Fanna and chided: "Fanna--you are a tattle tale."

"Just doing my job as your Guide. Remember how shaky you were when I brought you over?"

I felt guilty all of a sudden. You don't feel guilty or ashamed very long here. "I do appreciate everything you're doing for me, Fanna. I am grateful."

"I know, my dear." She made a pursy, it's-okay mouth. Her eyes turned back to Joe Viale, giving him the floor again (or the Street, as it were). What are any of our names in waking life? Who knows. Who cares. All that matters in dreams is the metaphor, the vision, the movie, the stage play, the molasses honey and syrupy flow of time like balmy mid afternoon air on a sunny, flawlessly blue-skied San Diego day. I have to wonder sometimes if San Diego itself is a construct of the dream world. Where are the boundaries between dreams and waking? Think about it. What is day dream and what is night dream? I can be so philosophical now that I have my espish power pack in the night world.

"How do you feel so far?" Joe Street or Viale said. He folded his pale, slightly hairy hands together over his lap. His fingers wrapped around a burgundy leather folder I had not noticed. Maybe my progress report was in it. Or maybe my first real mission?

"I am having a lot of fun."

"Good," he said heartily. Fanna beamed.

"I feel safe, happy, free--sometimes confused."

"That is normal," he said. "You are feeling all the right things. You should remember that I am a trained, licensed psychologist, and my concern for you is entirely professional. I wonder if you would tell me how you feel about your sexual immersion here."

I felt very relaxed, as if he'd suddenly given me a

tranquilizer, but without the dull narcotic cloud of minutes ago. "Very nice. I have been feeling my way around, so to speak." I wiggled my fingertips in the air. "I have that *Fingerspitzengefühl* (where did I learn German? How did I even know this was German for Finger Tip Feeling, as in The Expert Touch?) for quite a few male body surfaces. Very nice. It's almost like a hobby now, the way some people polish historical propeller planes and enjoy running their palms over those smooth, curvy surfaces."

He nodded, as if making notes in his book. "Metaphoric strength is sound. You are every bit the talented esper we measured. Very espish. Great metrics. Nice work, Fanna."

Fanna nodded in thanks, not saying anything.

Joe continued businesslike: "I thought very carefully. We feel that the earlier we explain the possibilities to you, the more likely you will be to join us as Fanna did."

"I am open to that," I said bravely and honestly. "I have fallen in love with this strange, powerful place or state of being or whatever it is."

"All of the above," Fanna said. "It's called Snow Globing." She extended a hand toward me, palm up, and a little snow globe appeared on it as if by magic. Well, the magic of dream land, that is. It was a glass hemisphere on a little wooden base. Inside, amid a sensuous bluish glow, was a tiny city with sky scrapers, even with windows in its towers. White flakes whirled and floated downward slowly in liquid. "We set up missions in dream lands like this. We go into small worlds like this, and do things to make the world a better place--usually by stroking the sensuous side of some strong but very dangerous person to make him be a better leader; or just some person whose slightest action can change history."

"Right," Joe said. "We carry on important missions for the government and for civilization. It's like a plate full of spinach. What we do is good for you, like eating spinach. But we enjoy it while we do so."

As he spoke, I could sense a great deal of adventure and wonderful events (including the most sensuous sex, enough to make you scream) ahead.

He continued: "I promise you, Rosemary Evening, that we will not rush you. We won't push you faster than you want to go. Life here gets a bit boring after a while. All those orgasms, all that balmy sunshine in the afternoon, all those fragrant rose gardens at night."

"I am still exploring," I countered.

"Yes," he said, "but again, we want to give you a reading into the next few chapters. The book goes on, and on, and on as long as you retain your passion. The work is never finished. When you have saved yourself, as you are on your way to doing, you may want to help others."

"I do."

"Nice. It will help you feel good. It will add new layers of self-confidence, pride, competence, whatever you want to call it. Your waking life will be yet again all the better for it."

I burst out laughing: "Do I go around grabbing men's balls on the bus and stuff?"

He and Fanna shook their heads, brightly. "Not at all. But your confidence is already way up, and so is the quality of your life. We can't talk about it here, Rosemary. You understand that."

"I don't want to."

"See," he said, shifting in his seat as if agitated, "even if I told you that you are a bright, pleasant young woman who had a horrific tragedy in your life--something nobody should have to suffer--you would forget about it a moment later." He snapped his fingers. For a moment, I almost had a sense of the dead weight around my soul, the anchor and chain pulling me down into a dark sea of unimaginable grief, the kind you feel at the loss of your only child. Whatever happened in my life, it was…

He snapped his fingers again, and I brightened. The dark feeling lifted. I felt like a swimmer bobbing to the surface after a near drowning incident. For a moment, I had been pulled down into the icy cold abyss the color of black ink. For a moment, something so unmentionably terrible had been pulling me down by the ankles. For an instant, I nearly glimpsed...why I had arrived here, sobbing and shaking, ready to melt in a puddle on the ground except Fanna helped me stay upright, back in that airlock...

He snapped his fingers a third time, and I shook off whatever it was. I bobbed to the surface with an enormous feeling of relief. I felt like a swimmer in an old travel poster, bobbing up like a cork in a one-piece swim suit, waving my arms as if swimming. My face glittered with sunshine, and a cool shore breeze ruffled my wet, flying hair (which was, curiously, cut in a dark page boy). But it's all metaphor, you see. Merrily, merrily, merrily, life is but a dream...

He nodded to Fanna, excusing us. "Rosemary, let us dance a little bit together."

"Oh?" I heard the light band music coming from the grand ballroom of the Hotel De Javu, which had been built in the 1880s and still captured that Victorian atmosphere. The band music was pre-jazz, pre-ragtime, and appeared to be light, pleasant chamber music of some type. No, it was a light waltz. It was like if you drank from a champagne bottle with the label Waltz on it, the word LITE would be printed over the word Waltz. It was all so flighty and immaterial and flittery and gay, like the Gay 1890s before they existed.

Joe Street was tall, and strong. He was kind of an iron man, in his dark gray suit that was cut and pressed tightly enough to cut paper. I happily leaned into him as he gently led me about. I felt his steel thigh against my feminine soft legs. I smiled happily up at him, and he beamed as he looked down those few inches. He had his right arm behind my back, with one hand resting on my waist in back. I wished he'd put it over my fanny. With his left hand, he held my soft hand out away from us as we twirled lightly to the music. I felt immensely happy and sexy in his arms. I leaned my cheek against the whipcord muscles of his right shoulder, which I could feel clearly through his suit. His grip against my back tightened.

"I wanted to have a moment alone with you to explain that your talent is such--your powers are such--that we can trust you in the future to take care of pressing missions for us. You see, we have people in the dream world who are more than just lost, broken souls. We have world leaders who dream and wander into this space. That is why this is such a top secret, hush hush Government project."

"Oh, Joe," I said, "you mean that the Clocktower Institute is a front for espionage and James Bond stuff?" I must have sounded thrilled, which I was.

He nodded. "Yes, Rosemary. Or should I say, Miss Evening?"

I giggled. "I am probably Mrs. Something in my waking condition. Am I not? I feel like a house wife or at least a married woman."

He gave me a veiled, affectionate, but secretive *smule* (which is a combination smürk + smile). I read in his eyes that I must never learn the truth about my daytime life. He almost sort of snapped his fingers in his eyes, if that makes any sense. He blinked at me, as if snapping his fingers again. It was a hypnotic, controlling, total gesture. I just wanted to melt into him, to dance and dance, to have an orgasm just throbbing together on that hard wood dance floor amid a kind of foggy light. I had no idea if others were dancing. Maybe it was 1888 and we had traveled in time. Who knows?

Joe held me tight, while looking down at me with that

bad boy grin.

Now he had both arms on my back. His strong hands held me to him by my shoulder blades. I put my palms up against the steely muscles of his chest. My fingers twitched involuntarily, surprised by the rock-hard curves of his chest muscles. In a kind of dream or swoon, I laid my cheek against his chest, hoping to hear his heart beating in the cage of his desire for me (or I imagined so).

He held me, and we swayed about in perfect unison. Without thinking about it, my right hand brushed downward. My fingertips explored the geography of his body, from his shirt down to the stiffer material of his trousers. My index finger located the dangling handle of his zipper. With two fingers, I pinched the handle and slipped it down as we continued gyrating.

"You have a rare talent," he whispered in my ear. I felt the warmth and wetness of his breath, and almost thought I felt the tip of his tongue in my ear. It was so sexy that I thrilled throughout my body. I felt long and slim in his arms, and his hands radiated appreciation as he held my narrow little shoulders against his powerful spread. My little fingers wiggled into the opening down there. My hand slid stealthy as a snake into the warmth of his underpants. Before I even got into that little opening in his cotton briefies, I could feel a massive hard-on waiting for me.

"Oh dear Rosemary," he said in a weak, overpowered voice. "Miss Evening."

My little fingers, almost pudgy and very sly, slipped through the last barrier and found themselves in the damp mass of his hair (which I could almost bet, sight unseen, was a wiry tangle of blackness shining almost gunmetal blue if I'd had a flashlight). My entire hand was just big enough to fit around that massive cock that rose like a tree trunk in the night.

What had Fanna once told me that a wise woman had

told her? That *...men are like wild animals. They are almost impossible to capture and tame... As long as you have a man's cock in your hand, he is helpless. It's like throwing a turtle on its back, or whatever the urban myth is, and the turtle can't move. It's like that with a man. If you can get your hands on his cock--to say nothing of your lips around it--he is putty in your hands.*

Dr. Street held me tightly in those steely arms, making me melt in his embrace. On we danced to the lilting, happy waltz music of long ago. I raised my face and pressed my cheek against his. He looked down, as if gravely, and pressed his cheek against mine. I felt prickly stubble--that five o'clock beard shadow--and smelled a faint aroma of soap and aftershave. His hair had a trace of something--what? An aroma of surfboard--about it, the way that is, composed of coconut, lime, and salt water combed by sea winds? I wanted to float away to some distant island with him and be the sand to his tide. I wanted to show off for a full, silvery, feminine moon as we stroked and poked in that mythical love beach. But I was getting ahead of myself, and that would not do.

For the moment it was enough to firmly grasp his steel cable cock in my hand, to be in control of it, and to anticipate the moment when I would get my mouth around its prow. So we danced gently together, he and I, swaying as we held each other, with my hand in the heat of his pants. I waited until I could not stand it any longer. I looked up at him with longing in my eyes. He read my desire, meeting it with devastation in his eyes. "You will do," he whispered tensely through gritted teeth. "Oh, Rosemary."

"You must have me," I said, the talented Miss Rosemary Evening.

"Yes," he said weakly as his right hand moved down from the small of my back to explore the cleft between my buttocks. I heard the sharp inhalation of shock and desire as his left hand closed around my tight and waiting buttock. My hand began gently stroking his cock, which grew more massive with each movement. He helped me out by spurting and dribbling in his need, so that I was able to twirl my hand gently and coat his member with its own warm cream.

"I want your cream inside me," I said. My voice must have been tense, because it sounded like a military command to my own ringing ears. My free hand explored up and down his body, ignoring his clothes as if they were not there. I was under his suit, pulling and undoing, yanking and spanking.

In a wink, we transported from the dance floor to a quiet place--his pad, I assume. It was one of these moneyed haunts draped in ivy and soft orangey coach lights. We fairly floated through the cute heavy oak door shaped like an iron standing on end (ogive, it's called). Down book-lined corridors we went, past something like a mead hall with heavy wooden chairs and a table like an aircraft carrier, down further, past a bath lined in tiny tiles so white they gleamed almost bluish, and into a bedroom with the most enormous four-poster bed I'd seen in a long time.

Joe shed his suit and clothing as we went, a talent men seem to have if they've been with a lot of women. He was no newbie. I still held his cock, and therefore I owned him. I was not about to let go.

What was I wearing? By then, he had dressed me as he wanted me to be in his own dream. I wore a filmy white gown with long, flowing sleeves. Under it I wore a softly padded white cotton bra with tiny flowers all over, and matching panties with an open crotch. What a nice touch. We floated onto the bed, with Joe leading, backwards, so he landed on his back with his legs in the air--slow motion falling, as if we were on the moon. "I want you over me," he said, pulling me by my free hand. I had to let go of his cock at that point. It stood up stiff as a ramrod, and he held it with his right hand, stroking it skillfully in practiced motions. If I had shoes, they fell away. I stood on the bed in white stocking-hose, letting him look under the dress, which he lifted with his other hand. I stood with my arms akimbo and turned slightly from side to side, oscillating to give him a view. I was sure by then that the crotch hole in my undies had become damp with my own eagerness for that beautiful prong.

"I want you to fill me up," I said in a challenging tone. Where did that come from? Where was the beaten, sobbing woman of a few weeks ago? "I want you to take that cock and press my lips apart. But first I want you to start kissing me from the ground up, and don't miss anything."

I thought he was going to cry, so mournful and yearning was his tone. "Oh Rosemary, please, let me lick your feet."

I was unrelenting. The bargain must be hard. "I will let you lick my feet if you watch me put my fingers in my pussy. I want to see if I am wet."

His only answer was a whimper. He crawled across the bed and held my one foot in both hands, as if it were a birdie that had fallen out of its nest in a tree and landed broken on the ground. So tenderly did he kiss my feet, licking the soles and working his way around my ankles, that I let out a groan of shock as I touched myself. My lips parted easily, so wet were they. I confess--I think I peed a few tiny spurts in my own excitement.

As I had told him, he watched with pleading, big dark eyes as I held my labia open with two fingers of one hand while I inserted two fingers of the other hand and felt my wet insides. As he mournfully looked, he held my toes in his mouth and sucked.

"Take off these stocking hose," I said. "I want to feel your tongue on my skin."

"Yes, Miss Evening." This panther of a man, this killer spy who was built like a steel motorcycle, rippling nakedly with muscles and covered with scrub brush black hairs, crawled around the base of my legs and started to pull down my stocking hose. Then he grew stubborn. "No! I want to taste you through the slit." He yanked my hose back up, violently.

I closed my eyes at the thought and felt all my strength ebb away. "Yes" was all I could say, weakly. I was afraid I might fall over.

"Stay where you are," he ordered. "Rosemary Evening, I am going to suck your pussy. You will be strong and remain standing."

Even so, I leaned awkwardly with my fingertips on his automobile back while he raised his head up under the dress and found the weakness of my life.

"Oh," I moaned, long and brokenly, as he used his finger tips to pull apart that long slit. I felt his lips on my lips, nuzzling me. I felt faint. I have little danglers down there, like little steaks, juicy and good to suck, and he tenderly kneaded them with his teeth and lips. I felt electric needles prickling through my outer cunt lips. I wanted to reach down, pull up the dress, and help him by reaching into my wetness, but more so I wanted him to do this to me. I wanted this done to me. He must be in charge now. He must accomplish this mission. I felt tender and worshipful. I wanted to adore him. I wanted to treat him as the man he was, every inch of him. He lived up to his promise, and more. I would love him forever (or whatever passes for that in a dream).

He licked his way around, holding the panties apart. It felt very sexy to be tongue-fucked through my panties. The slit in them was made exactly for this; well, maybe to pee through also. I did not fancy him to be a golden showers kind of guy.

When I could stand it no longer, I sank onto the bed

backwards, cushioning my fall with my fingertips and then my elbows. Joe never relented, but kept licking away. I felt his tongue like an electric eel, running up and down on my inner lips. He flicked my pee hole until it tingled and my body began twitching with a really huge orgasm. Then he attacked my clit, licking counter-clockwise with that magnificent tongue. It was like being a clock and being wound up. He knew exactly what to do. I lay with my knees apart, moaning and holding myself open while he ravaged my interior.

But I knew the best was yet to come. Like a pirate boarding his ship, he walked into me on his knees. He held his cannon in both hands. It was so stiff and hard it did not waggle but pointed straight at me. I cried out: "Oh yes, Joe, Joe, push it in. Spread me. I want to feel you inside me."

He wasted no time, except for the moment when his head touched the wet tangle of my lips. I helped, pulling him in with one hand while spreading myself open with the other. When I felt that mighty truck pushing--everything changed. I felt full at last. I surrendered to his majesty and cried for him to do what he wished. He moaned with me, as if we were in chorus. He hooked his forearms under my knees. I was helpless as he hoisted my legs high so that my feet waggled limply behind him.

He began really pounding me now. The bed creaked and groaned. I bounced on the mattress. Each massive thrust hit me with a loud slap and I went flying. But he held me by my thighs, while I braced myself with my palms flat on the bed. Wham, wham, wham, in rapid succession, he pounded me while his own cries rose in pitch and desperation. His passion inflamed me, and I had to bite the knuckles of one hand to keep myself from shrieking. My knuckles grew wet and dripped saliva, while my other hand held me open so Joe could reach his climax and take me with him. Orgasm after orgasm rippled through my body, making my flesh quiver in rapid pulses. But Joe was heading toward the massive one, and I bated my breath attentively. I studied him closely, watching every sign in his facial expression, in his powerful arms and shoulders, in his flat washboard abs, in his powerful football player thighs, as he mounted me like we were two animals. When he came, he let out a series of "Oh, oh!" shouts and I sobbed for joy as fire blazed through me. I was burning up. My body was taken and thrown with electricity, with lightning. He was the thunder. My final massive orgasm was the lightning. We collapsed together and lay motionless, breathing together as one person.

I stroked his arms and his belly gently, waiting for his breathing to subside. He was a powerful beast with a lot of appetite left. He kissed me, gathering his strength. Oh wow, was he going for more? I was helpless, but hungry. Yes. He pulled back and lifted one of my legs, sucking on the toes. I squealed with pleasure, feeling tickled. I offered my other foot, stroking his nose playfully, until he snatched it and stuffed those toes into his mouth. He alternated feet, making love to them, while I reached down and stroked his dick. He was hard again, magnificently so, and while he played with my toes, making me tingle, I moved down and enveloped his beautiful pink prong. He went all the way inside me, and I could just stroke the base of his cock with my thumb and two fingers.

Gaining energy, he laid my legs down together on his left. Grabbing the curvy fullness of my left hip, he forced me to roll over so that my ass spread under his eager, starving gaze. He pawed my buttocks with his palms, while tonguing my cleft and both holes in wild, noisy lunges. He held me apart while he kissed and licked and sucked at me. My pendants were electric again. My holes were open for him. I reached back and held my cheeks apart while he kneed his way in and ass fucked me. The pain was exquisite for a minute or so until I grew limp and open for him. Making me powerless and adoring me at the same time, he pounded at me. I could hear his breath building in raspy croaks while he labored at me, and I just loved the pounding. I wailed for more and more and more. I cried out to him "Yes yes yes oh yeah all the way do it take me do whatever pleases you because it makes me feel so good."

He came again, and sank down on my back, tenderly favoring my long, lean waist with eager hands. I submitted to his gentle attentions, knowing I had brought him to this. I had the talent and the hand in his pants. As long as you have your hand on his cock, a man is your helpless victim. He is your accomplice. He does your bidding. You give yourself to him taking you as you give yourself as he takes you in an endless cycle of joy and anticipation. It is a feast of the senses--especially when you are free like I have become in the dream reality that occupies one third of our lives--maybe more if you count day dreaming and wishful thinking.

As we lay together quietly in the comforting gloom, I pressed my index finger against his nose. "Well, Mr. Street, do you suppose I will be able to handle the missions coming up?"

He was still a bit breathless, panting: "Oh yeah. You are indeed the Talented Miss Rosemary Evening. I would trust you with my life."

"At least the one third sleep cycle of your life," I teased.

"And you are the Funny Miss Rosemary Evening," he said. "I want to hang on to you."

"I will stay with the team," I promised carefully, not wanting to seem too eager or too easy.

He lay beside me, resting his head on an elbow and a hand so they made a triangle. I smelled the pheromones in his armpit hair, and impulsively licked him there. He reacted like a man being tickled, squirming. I told him: "Maybe if you're good, we'll do this again some time."

He took a turn at pressing my nose with his finger. "You go off and play some more, Rosemary Evening. You still have a lot of learning to do. But don't worry--I'll be calling you before you know it."

"Will we be storming any beaches?" I murmured amid our communal drunken passion.

"Maybe some bitches," he quipped amid the same lethargy that overtook us both.

"Then I have lot to look forward to," I said, settling back. "I'd prefer Butches, as in guys with crew cuts or something. You can have the bitches, Joe."

He chose not to keep the line of puns going, for fear, I suppose, of getting into deep water. Instead, he fell asleep with his cheek against my shoulder and a smile on his face, while I held my arm around his head and nuzzled close.

And then I woke up.

That's all there is for now, until my next dream, and I hope you will join me, and Joe, and Fanna, and the other members (no pun intended) of a growing team as we fight for truth, justice, and apple pie.

More Info: Clocktower Books
= online since 1996 =

Clocktower Books was, to our knowledge, the world's first publisher ever to publish real digital, proprietary (not public domain), novel-length fiction (books, novels) online in digital format for download (as opposed to CD-Rom and other portable formats). See the Clocktower Books website and museum for more information about our distinguished, innovative, and pioneering history that continues today and into the future.

We launched our original program in spring 1996, using an innovative process of publishing weekly serial chapters. Readers who needed to know the outcome, and couldn't stand the suspense, could email for a complete digital text file anywhere in the world. We received raves and kudos from around the globe.

We used this serial chapter method to publish three John Argo books over 1996-1996: *This Shoal of Space* and *Pioneers* (both SF); and *Neon Blue*, a suspense novel. All three novels were bestsellers in the earliest e-book forums, including the original Barnes & Noble website in 2000, and other venues including Rocket eBooks. See the publisher website for more info:

www.clocktowerbooks.com.

Look for announcements and other releases at Clocktower Books.

And more… the best is yet to come.

About Venti Editions

In early 2017, we introduced the Venti line of Clocktower Books. These are the new books, driven by digital technology, and no longer locked into the old technology-based definitions of short stories (print magazine) or novels (print book).

Venti means Twenty or Winds. Either way, a new wind is blowing (to quote Bob Dylan), and the middle length is open to anything longer than an old-fashioned short story and shorter than an old-fashioned print book (60,000 words on up).

Naturally, we'll pass along the great pricing you expect in a shorter, faster, better Venti Print edition. That term, by the way, we borrowed from a NASA concept—didn't work out so well for the space program, but works great for Venti publishing. To the stars, then!

About Clocktower Books

Our excellent authors include Renee Horowitz (*Pharmacy Sleuth Trilogy*); Robin Marchesi (*A Small Journal of Heroin Addiction*, a poetic autobiography in a post-Beat tradition); Dennis Latham (*The Bad Season*); Deborah Cannon (*Raven Trilogy*); and others including our Teenage Novelist/Poet. To learn about our latest offerings, please visit the website at

www.clocktowerbooks.com

Clocktower Books, a pioneering Internet, e-book, and San Diego small press publisher, launched in April 1996 by publishing the world's first entire (not partial) proprietary (not public domain) novels (long works, industry standard) for reading online in HTML format (not for reading on portable media like CD-ROM, floppies, or other intermediary media). Some reviewers are confused and think Gutenberg did this first, but they specialize in public domain. We were the first (John Argo: Neon Blue, This Shoal of Space, Pioneers; John T. Cullen: The Generals of October) to publish proprietary novels as noted.

Clocktower Books Museum Site

You will find at the Museum Pages on our website a detailed history of our pioneering publishing house starting from 1996—including references and documentation (ever a work in progress).

museum.clocktowerbooks.com

From 1998 to 2007, Clocktower Books also published what was, during its decade-long run, the world's first professional Web-only (online) magazine of speculative and dark fiction (or SFFH). We published new authors as well as officers and top names of the Science Fiction Writers of America (SFWA); more on our pioneering work at the Science Fiction Encyclopedia online (look under Far Sector).

Our magazine's major names over the years included Deep Outside SFFH and Far Sector SFFH. We published many nominees or later awardees of the Hugo, Nebula, Sturgeon, and other global awards including British, Canadian, and Australian. The leading SF magazine historian Mike Ashley (Liverpool University Press) has stated he will recognize our pioneering magazine in the final volume of his authoritative SF magazine histories. We are mentioned in the SF Encyclopedia.

John Argo and Clocktower Books Present

Stunning and poetic far-future history by John Argo in the tradition of Cordwainer Smith's Classic Norstrilia and other tales of the Instrumentality.

Moon Berry Wine: Far Future SF

CLOCKTOWER BOOKS

Science Fiction Novel by John Argo in the Empire of Time Series

Jean-Thomas Cullen and Clocktower Books Present

A sentimental, clean romantic story set in contemporary Connecticut. A young war widow has become a Sleeping Beauty, stung by the loss of her soldier husband, and works as a librarian in the tiny town of Emery. One hot summer day, just looking for a cool spot while his car is fixed, Prince Charming stops by in the form of a young millionaire who has suffered a painful divorce and isn't really looking for love. Neither is she. But old Cupid shoots them both with his arrows, and the ground moves beneath their feet...

Valley of Seven Castles: Progressive Thriller

Set in tomorrow's Europe, in a world gone global and run as one big feudal state by a thousand zillionaire families, here is the world's first progressive thriller. A U.S. Army deserter running from a crime he didn't commit, and a young California woman who sold herself into a modern form of five-year slavery to pay her mother's final hospital bills, are on the run. With them they carry the plans for a new warplane fuselage that must not fall into the wrong hands. Chasing them from Paris to Luxembourg is the Chinese billionaire who murdered a young Luxembourg engineer in London and wants his toy back. In the spirit of John Buchan's 1915 *The Thirty-Nine Steps* as well as Alfred Hitchcock's 1935 movie version *The 39 Steps*, plus a big surprise (see Thrillerology in the novel). Add to that the pace of the 2002 thriller movie The Bourne Identity starring Matt Damon and Franka Potente, based on a 1970 thriller novel by Robert Ludlum, and you have a first-class read.

(see opposite page for cover image)

Valley of Seven Castles

A Luxembourg Thriller by John T. Cullen

PROGRESSIVE THRILLERS SERIES

Here's a thriller unlike anything you've ever read. Think of the dark comedy movie After Hours (Martin Scorsese, all-star cast) which is considered one of the funniest (and craziest) films ever made. We agree. Think of Linda Fiorentino in The Last Seduction, Jack Lemmon in The Out-of-Towners, and how about Thomas Pynchon's classic novel The Crying of Lot 49. YANAPOP (stands for Young Adult, New Adult, Participating Older Persons) is the name of a giant (fictional) entertainment corporation in Los Angeles. It's the love story of Martin Brown and Chloë Setreal, and how Martin became Odysseus in his insane and dangerous journey to reach his Penelope.

Nonfiction by John T. Cullen: Dead Move

John T. Cullen, a San Diego author and scholar (BA, BBA, MS) applies his journalistic and historical expertise to solve a long-standing true crime. During Thanksgiving Week 1892, a stylish young woman (about 24) officially called The Beautiful Stranger by the Hotel del Coronado near San Diego, checked in under a false name and died a violent, mysterious death a few days later. Her case became a national sensation full of notoriety overnight because of allegations of affairs with men in high places. It was a Victorian scandal of epic proportions, resulting in the famous ghost legend at the hotel. John T. Cullen, basing his research entirely on true history (no ghosts were harmed), provides the first ever plausible explanation of what really happened—including a coverup of global proportions. See also Lethal Journey, the noir gaslight mystery thriller he wrote to dramatize *Dead Move*, on which *Lethal Journey* is closely based. You have the option of buying both books under one cover, titled *Coronado Mystery* (a package deal).

(see next two pages for cover images)

Coronado Mystery

by JOHN T. CULLEN

2 great books in 1

Dead Move & Lethal Journey

1892 GASLIGHT MYSTERY

San Diego's notorious true crime
enigma solved - ghost legend

THE BEAUTIFUL STRANGER

* her violent mysterious death *

Thriller by John T. Cullen: Lethal Journey

Closely based on his nonfictional scholarly analysis of the 1892 true crime (*Dead Move*) here is a dramatization treated as a gaslight era noir suspense thriller.

Ray Bradbury Loved This One:

Ray Bradbury wrote a personal fan mail note to John T. Cullen in January 2008, praising this little gem, a novel that is a tribute both to Charles Dickens' classic A Christmas Carol, and to Ray Bradbury's dark but playful fantasies.

Lots More Where These Came From...

Please visit the website of Clocktower Books for a full listing of our exciting fiction and nonfiction books, articles, and short works by a variety of talented authors.

www.clocktowerbooks.com

Look for Upcoming Great Venti Editions

Venti means twenty. The intermediate length of Venti edition may run anywhere from about 20,000 to 50,000 words. Take our word for it!

We will be releasing Venti Editions in SF, Suspense, Thriller, Romantic, and Literary fiction lines. We will also release longer nonfiction works as Venti Nonfiction. Please drop in often, stay tuned, and prepare to enjoy thrills without end.